"It's obvious you've b
her."

Mackenzie was crouching to pet Tulip. Cade hadn't seen her since the previous week's training session, and he wanted to ask her how her day was and listen to everything on her mind.

"Tulip's training is coming along fine," Mackenzie said, rising. "No need to worry. She'll be ready soon."

"We couldn't be happier to have you here, Mackenzie," Mom said cheerily.

Cade almost raised his eyebrows at her use of the word *we*, but he didn't. He *was* happy to have her there. Even if it made him uncomfortable at times.

Mackenzie was transparent. What you saw was what you got. Cade, on the other hand, hid himself behind a socially acceptable exterior. And lately, he'd been tempted to let down his guard. Allow Mackenzie to catch a glimpse of the real him, the one he'd been trying to hide since New York. He had a feeling she'd already glimpsed it, but if she hadn't? She'd hate that side of him as much as he did.

Jill Kemerer writes novels with love, humor and faith. Besides spoiling her mini dachshund and keeping up with her busy kids, Jill reads stacks of books, lives for her morning coffee and gushes over fluffy animals. She resides in Ohio with her husband and two children. Jill loves connecting with readers, so please visit her website, jillkemerer.com, or contact her at PO Box 2802, Whitehouse, OH 43571.

Books by Jill Kemerer

Love Inspired

Wyoming Legacies

The Cowboy's Christmas Compromise
United by the Twins
Training the K-9 Companion

Wyoming Ranchers

The Prodigal's Holiday Hope
A Cowboy to Rely On
Guarding His Secret
The Mistletoe Favor
Depending on the Cowboy
The Cowboy's Little Secret

Visit the Author Profile page at LoveInspired.com for more titles.

Training the K-9 Companion

JILL KEMERER

LOVE INSPIRED

INSPIRATIONAL ROMANCE

LOVE INSPIRED®
INSPIRATIONAL ROMANCE

ISBN-13: 978-1-335-59746-5

Training the K-9 Companion

Copyright © 2024 by Ripple Effect Press, LLC

Recycling programs
for this product may
not exist in your area.

Love Inspired
22 Adelaide St. West, 41st Floor
Toronto, Ontario M5H 4E3, Canada
www.LoveInspired.com

Printed in Lithuania

MIX
Paper | Supporting
responsible forestry
FSC® C021394

And therefore will the Lord wait,
that he may be gracious unto you, and therefore
will he be exalted, that he may have mercy upon you:
for the Lord is a God of judgment:
blessed are all they that wait for him.
—*Isaiah* 30:18

To everyone taking a leap of faith.
I know all about starting over someplace new.
May the Lord bless you.

Chapter One

As usual, the restlessness snuck up on him, and, too late, Cade Moulten realized his mistake. Offering to help his mother train a therapy dog was just another attempt to atone for his past.

He couldn't back out now. He wouldn't if he could. Cade had other reasons—good ones—for being here.

"It's not much to look at, is it?" His mother, Christy Moulten, sat in the passenger seat of his truck and stared at the small industrial building with faded gray aluminum siding. Next to it, a matching structure roughly three times its size shared the parking lot. The early June sunshine began to fade as the day wound down.

Cade cut the engine, and his mom bent to pick up her purse. A few months shy of turning sixty-four, his mother hadn't slowed a bit. Her stylish blond bob, subtle makeup and smile lines gave her the appearance of someone who enjoyed life, but she also had a stubborn streak wider than a country mile.

At thirty-five, he'd mellowed to the point of not minding driving her around town whenever her driver's license was suspended—and that was often—nor did he mind living with her in the big house on the ranch. Kept her out of trouble.

Maybe they kept each other out of trouble.

He pocketed his keys. "What's it supposed to look like? It's a vet clinic, not a spa, Ma."

Cade had personally taken a loss on this property by selling it to the new veterinarian and her father for pennies on the dollar. Anything to convince a vet to take a chance on moving to Jewel River. When Dr. Bill Banks, the only veterinarian within two hours of here, retired last fall, it had affected every rancher and pet owner in this swath of Wyoming.

Jewel River needed a veterinarian ASAP.

Cade needed one, too. For his ranch and to be on call when Moulten Stables opened this fall. Ideally, his new horse-boarding venture would have an equine-certified vet, but they were hard to come by in rural Wyoming. Any animal doctor was. How much experience did the new vet have with horses?

"I don't know." Mom's nose crinkled in distaste as she shrugged. "I was hoping she'd have a nice sign and a few potted flowers to make the entrance more inviting. The beat-up siding and chain-link fence surrounding the property leaves a lot to be desired."

"Cut her some slack. The clinic isn't even open for business. She could be waiting for her father to arrive before updating the exterior. He's going to have plenty of renovations in order to turn that old warehouse into a service-dog training center."

"I suppose it doesn't matter. I'm thankful she found us a dog and is helping us train it. When I think of how happy it will make your grandmother and all the other nursing-home residents to have a dog visit them…well, I can't wait to get started. Plus, I miss having a dog around to spoil."

Cade wouldn't argue with that. Trudy Moulten was his only living grandparent, and he'd always been close to his paternal grandmother. She'd blanketed him and his younger brother, Ty, with love, affection and homemade treats as they were growing up and into adulthood. He couldn't count how many times she'd pointed him back to Jesus when he was getting in trouble.

He'd gotten in trouble a lot.

Probably would still be getting into trouble if his days on Wall Street hadn't ended so abruptly.

He stepped out of the truck at the same time his mother did. Their doors shut in unison, and they walked together across old blacktop with the occasional weed popping through.

He wished Nana hadn't broken a hip and become wheelchair bound. Ever since she'd moved into the nursing home last year, her dementia from Alzheimer's had been rapidly progressing. The doctors said she was entering the moderately severe stage. The impractical side of Cade hoped the comfort of having a therapy dog visiting her on a regular basis would slow the progress. The practical side of him knew it wouldn't make much of a difference. The dog would bring her joy, though, and that alone would make these training sessions worthwhile.

Besides, his late father would want him to help. Pete Moulten had been gone for six years now, and Cade missed him every day. The last time they'd been together, Cade had been living the high life in New York City. The memories of Dad's visit would always sting. Words had been said. Feelings hurt. Not long after, his father had died unexpectedly from an aggressive cancer they'd known nothing about. And ever since, Cade had been trying to be a man his father would be proud of, the one he'd raised him to be.

He'd never be that man.

He'd made mistakes. Mistakes no one knew about. Mistakes he didn't want anyone to know about.

Most people around here saw him as a successful rancher and a financial genius who'd climbed the ladder of Wall Street by the age of twenty-eight. None of them knew what a slippery climb it had been. And he hoped they'd never find out.

"What kind of dog do you think she picked out for us?" Mom paused when they reached the front door.

"Hopefully, a golden retriever. They're friendly and easy to be around." He held the door open for her, and she went inside.

"But they shed something terrible. I was thinking more along the lines of a cocker spaniel. Smaller. Less difficult for me to handle."

"I guess we'll find out."

"I guess so," Mom said. "She said to go straight to the back."

A construction zone greeted them, and they made their way through a small waiting room and unfinished reception area to proceed down a hall with several doors on either side. Cade assumed they were examination rooms. At the end of the hall, they went through another door and emerged into a large, open warehouse space. Empty kennels in a variety of sizes were stacked haphazardly on the concrete floor as if they'd recently been unpacked.

And then Cade saw her. Mackenzie Howard—Dr. Mackenzie Howard—the woman he'd talked to on the phone several times last summer in the hopes she'd take a chance and move to their town. Thankfully, she'd left Cheyenne to start her own practice right here in Jewel River.

He hadn't expected Mackenzie to be around his age. Hadn't realized she'd be so tall. So assured. So absolutely stunning.

Why he'd pictured her in her late forties, he couldn't say. Her slightly husky voice perhaps? The woman striding their way had long strawberry blond hair, hooded midnight blue eyes, high cheekbones, thin lips and a row of not-quite-straight white teeth. She was wearing jeans, a gray T-shirt and athletic shoes.

Her style was simple. Unfussy. If she had on any makeup, he couldn't detect it.

"Hi there." She stopped near where they were standing.

"You must be Christy. I'm Mackenzie." She held out her hand, and his mom shook it and sandwiched Mackenzie's with her other one.

"It is such a pleasure to meet you," Mom said. "Should I call you Dr. Howard?"

Her throaty chuckle hit Cade in the gut. Gorgeous and unpretentious. Not a good combination if he wanted to avoid trouble. And he did want to avoid trouble. He hadn't dated in a good long while, and he planned on keeping it that way. His ethical lapse at his job in the city had made him question his values. How could he be sure he wouldn't mess up again?

He couldn't. And until he was sure he had integrity, he refused to get close to a woman. It would only end badly.

"Call me Mackenzie."

"Okay." Mom shifted and smiled at him. "This is my son Cade."

"We finally meet." Mackenzie thrust her hand to him.

"Nice to meet you." A prickly feeling simmered at the base of his neck as he shook her hand.

"Yeah," she said with a grin, "I feel like we're old buddies after all the conversations we had last year."

Buddies? She might think they were pals, but his pulse didn't race like this when he was around his friends.

He gave her a controlled smile. "We're glad you're finally here."

"I'm glad to be here. Dad can't wait to join me. Only a few more weeks of traveling and he'll move here for good."

Last September, Cade had tried to convince her to relocate to Jewel River, but she'd insisted on waiting until her father could come, too. As a trainer of service dogs, her dad traveled to teach people with disabilities how to handle their new dogs, and Mackenzie had decided to work temporarily with a large animal veterinarian in Montana to get acquainted with the typical problems ranchers faced.

Personally, Cade was glad she'd brushed up on large animal care. He had a gut feeling the luxury vacation companies he was courting to winter their horses with Moulten Stables would expect him to have a vet available with extensive experience treating horses. Without their business, he might not be able to offer low rates to the locals. One of the reasons he was opening the stables was to provide horses for rent to teens who wanted to join the rodeo team.

"Well, we're thrilled to have you." His mom beamed. A cautionary tingle went down his spine. His mother was a confirmed matchmaker. She'd been trying to get "her boys" married off for years. She'd only stopped badgering Ty after he'd gotten engaged, but Zoey had died from cystic fibrosis before the wedding. That had been almost five years ago. Ty hadn't been the same since.

And that meant their mother focused her matchmaking efforts on Cade.

Christy considered any single woman a potential bride. And by any, he meant *any.* Only a few months ago, his mother had casually tried to set him up on a date with a recently divorced school librarian who was ten years older than him and had four kids. Cade sighed. Mackenzie had no idea what was about to hit her.

"Are you ready to meet your new dog?" Mackenzie's hands were in the prayer position near her chest.

"Yes." Mom's eyes sparkled. Whether it was from the thought of seeing the dog, the idea of him and Mackenzie together, or both, Cade didn't know, nor did he care.

He never should have offered to join her for these training sessions.

Do it for Nana.

He mentally girded himself. *Fine.* It would be worth the discomfort if it meant bringing even a smidgeon of joy to Nana's life.

It wasn't as if he'd had a choice in the matter, anyhow. Two weeks ago, Mom had attempted to park in front of Annie's Bakery. Her car had jumped the curb and ended up partially on the sidewalk. Sheriff Smith had caught her in the act. There went her license for another ninety days.

Cade *had* to drive her here. Ubers and taxis weren't a thing in Jewel River.

Mackenzie disappeared through the door into the clinic area. Cade didn't even peek at his mother. If he saw the gleaming, scheming, wedding-dreaming expression on her face—the one that said she'd found Cade's bride—he would lose his temper and get into it with her right there.

Not happening.

In no time at all, Mackenzie returned with the smallest, fluffiest dog he'd ever seen. She kept a firm hold on its leash as it pranced their way.

His mother gasped, bringing her hands to her mouth. Then she crouched as the little peach fluffball spun in circles before her.

"This is Tulip." Mackenzie smiled.

"Are you sure this is the right one?" Cade squinted at the pint-size ball of fuzz. He wiped his palm down his cheek. "I've seen raccoons three times its size."

His mom rose and shifted to stand next to Mackenzie. They gave him identical glares.

Double trouble.

That right there was a problem. His mom was bad enough. Cade had a feeling Mackenzie was equally formidable.

"Is she a Pomeranian?" His mother turned to Mackenzie.

"Yes, she's three years old. Her former owner was an elderly woman who passed away. Her son couldn't keep the dog, so a local animal shelter took her in. Dad has a number of contacts who call him when they have a dog with potential to be a therapy or service dog."

"Where has she been staying?" Cade asked. "Tulip, right?"

"Yes, Tulip. She's been staying with me. She's a sweetheart. Very in tune with people's moods, and she's surprisingly mellow for a toy breed."

Tulip trotted on tiny legs over to him. Her face was cute. Big brown eyes. He bent and let the dog sniff his hand. She nudged the side of it with her little brown nose, and he chuckled. "You want me to pet you, huh?"

Her tongue stuck out as if to say yes. Her pale peach fur was as soft as it looked. She ate up the attention.

"I've been working with her on basic commands," Mackenzie said. "She's smart. A fast learner. She has a few bad habits, but I think she'll overcome them with time. Tulip, come." Tulip immediately turned and headed toward her. She gave the dog a small treat and patted her head. Mackenzie handed Christy the leash. "Here, I'll let you get to know her."

Within seconds, his mom scooped up Tulip and petted her. The dog twisted to lick her face, and she laughed.

"Actually, Christy, that's one of the behaviors I'm trying to stop. Tulip is not allowed to lick faces." Mackenzie sounded pleasant enough, but Cade recognized the strength in her tone.

"She's just giving me a little kiss." Mom hugged the dog and set her back on the ground.

"When you take her to the nursing home, she can't lick the residents' faces. She needs to be calm, sit nicely and allow them to pet her."

"That's all well and good, but I'll be her owner, her person, her mommy." She gave Mackenzie a pointed look. Cade's eyelid started doing the flickering thing it did whenever she used that tone.

"I can see we have a lot to cover." Mackenzie shrugged pleasantly. "While Tulip is very cute, she isn't a baby or a child. She's a mature dog, and we're going to have expectations for her. You'll work with her at home, and each week I'll give you more instructions. Six weeks should be enough to train her to be a therapy dog. Like I said, she's very smart. My dad is qualified to do the certification testing for her to become a Canine Good Citizen. She's a bright little pup."

"Six weeks, huh?" Mom couldn't take her eyes off Tulip.

"If you work with her at home, yes."

"I suppose you're going to tell me she can't sleep with me." She looked crestfallen.

"Her crate would be best at night. During the day, you'll want to spend plenty of time with her and give her lots of attention and affection. In the meantime, we can go over the basic commands she already knows, and then we can load up your car with her supplies." Mackenzie gave Cade a confused glance. "You're welcome to stay here with us or wait in the reception area. It's up to you."

"What? Oh, no, Mackenzie." Mom shook her head with an amused smile. "Cade is going to be learning everything, too. Since Tulip will be living with both of us, it's best we're on the same page. He volunteered, didn't you?"

At least his mom hadn't pinched his cheeks during her speech. He didn't have a chance to answer because Mackenzie spoke first. "I'm afraid I'm missing something. Are you two sharing the dog? I don't know about her living in two separate homes."

"No, no, nothing like that. Cade and I live together." To his horror, Mom came over to him and wrapped her arm around his waist, then leaned her cheek against his upper arm.

Mackenzie's eyes widened, and her mouth formed an O.

Cade didn't embarrass easily. In fact, not much fazed him. But the flames licking his neck had to be turning his cheeks brick red. This was *not* the first impression he wanted to make with Mackenzie. Did she think he was a mama's boy?

A slew of justifications came to mind.

My dad died, and I'm looking out for my mother. I need to live at the ranch because I'm in charge of it. I'm independently wealthy, not sponging off my mom. Her driver's license was suspended for the seven hundredth time, and I'm making life easier on myself by joining her since I have to drive her anyway.

"We'll both be training Tulip," he said. Why explain anything more? It would serve no purpose. Besides, none of those things were the full truth.

Helping train Tulip was another attempt to be a good guy. But he wasn't. The vain, insecure side of him was still there. He'd been trying to bury it ever since his father passed away.

No sense in dwelling on the past. He just wanted this meet and greet with the dog to be over.

While she was certain Tulip would thrive with the Moultens, Mackenzie wasn't convinced Christy had what it would take to train Tulip to be a therapy dog. The next six weeks would prove it one way or the other. But that was the least of her worries at the moment. She'd never been the sole veterinarian of a community before, and she wasn't certain she was ready to treat large animals. Small ones? No problem. But emergency surgery on a cow or a horse? Questionable.

She'd done her best to put the past behind her, but the C-section gone wrong on a family's beloved horse during her residency was always there like a rock lodged in her gut. She'd never forget the children's wails or the lawsuit that followed. She'd been cleared of wrongdoing, but the emotional damage remained. All these years later and she still got nervous at the thought of repeating that nightmare.

Mackenzie motioned for Cade to follow her to one of the patient rooms where she'd stored all of Tulip's supplies. It had taken only twenty minutes to show the mother-and-son duo the basic commands to use with Tulip. As much as Mackenzie had enjoyed meeting them both, she was dying to check out every nook and cranny of the trailer she'd had outfitted to be her mobile vet clinic, which had arrived only an hour ago.

Cade—all six muscular and rugged feet of him—followed closely behind her, throwing her off slightly. And that in itself was strange. Yes, like most women, she appreciated a fine-looking man, but at thirty-two, she didn't see herself finding *the one*.

Her life wasn't exactly conducive to romance. In Cheyenne, she and the senior vet had split the on-call duties. Here? She'd be the only veterinarian for miles, and she anticipated being on call 24-7. Plus, she wasn't girlie. She liked jeans and sweats and old T-shirts. Her beauty routine consisted of brushing her hair and swiping on lip gloss. Occasionally, she'd braid her hair. Anything more seemed too fancy.

In addition to the no-time factor, she couldn't seem to shake her skeptical nature. She blamed her mother for that. How many times had Bonnie Howard disappeared from her life, only to show up unannounced, claiming she missed Mackenzie, and then vanish a few weeks later after Mackenzie had loaned her money that was never repaid? Too many to count.

It had been three years since she'd seen her mother. She counted it as a blessing.

Her parents had divorced when she was ten, and after a

few years of the nomad lifestyle with her mom, Mackenzie had insisted on living with her father full-time. Best decision she'd ever made.

"Here we are." Mackenzie opened the door to the second room on the left. "I packed her crate with treats, toys, food dishes, a therapy-dog vest, harness—you name it. Oh, and here's her doggy booster seat for the car." Mackenzie reached for the crate's handle at the same time Cade did. Their hands touched. She almost dropped the handle.

Yes, it had been too long since she'd been on a date. She'd forgotten what it was like to be attracted to a man. Cade threw her off-balance. And she didn't need anything else disrupting her life at the moment.

"I've got it." His cowboy hat tipped forward, shading his eyes. She'd discretely checked him out earlier when he'd taken off said cowboy hat. He had dark blue eyes and short, tousled dark blond hair. A straight nose, full eyebrows, broad shoulders. His expensive brand of jeans fit him well.

"I thought you'd be older," she blurted out. But then, she tended to say whatever was on her mind.

A grin slowly spread across his face. "I thought you would be, too."

"I get that." She lifted a shoulder in a shrug. "It's my voice. Raspy."

"I like it."

He did? Mackenzie had no idea how to respond, so she regrouped, pointing to the unopened bag of food nearby. "Um, there's her food. One cup a day. No more."

"Got it. Is this it?" He hauled the large bag onto his shoulder as if it weighed no more than a pillow. The crate dangled from his other hand.

"Yes. That should do it. Here, I'll show you how to install the booster seat in your car." She headed to the doorway, taking care not to touch him as she passed by. The faint scent of his cologne added to his masculine appeal.

Until now, she hadn't really thought about Cade Moulten beyond the fact he was the one who'd convinced her to start a new practice here and had sold her and her father this property. But now that they were face-to-face?

She had questions. Ones she wouldn't ask. An internet search would be a better place to start.

Later.

"How much experience do you have with horses?" he asked as they continued down the hallway to the back room.

The question made her uneasy. Had he found out about the incident where she'd lost both the mother and foal? The lawsuit was public record. Her acquittal was, too.

"I've worked with horses. Not a lot. Why?" She glanced back at him.

"I'm in the process of opening a horse-boarding facility on the outskirts of town, and I need to have an experienced vet on call."

She opened the door to the back room for him. The past months had boosted her confidence in treating horses. Eventually, she might even enjoy it. She'd always wanted a horse of her own. Had ridden plenty of her friends' horses as a teen. But until she faced an emergency with a large animal, she couldn't say for sure if she'd be up to the task. Only time would tell.

"I'm pretty much on call for everyone in the surrounding area. I know the basics—I'm licensed to treat large and small animals—but I've been treating mostly pets for the past several years. If you need an expert, I suggest finding someone else."

His jaw seemed to jut out. Stubborn…like his mother. Mackenzie wasn't fooled by Christy's warm, welcoming demeanor. The woman knew how to get her way. Mackenzie admired her for it.

"All set?" Christy, holding Tulip in her arms, beamed and joined them as they continued to the door leading outside. On the blacktop, Mackenzie gave the trailer a longing glance, then followed Cade to his truck.

"I just love our little princess," Christy said. Tulip licked her face again. Mackenzie would have to ignore it for now.

Cade's truck looked top-of-the-line and brand-new. He didn't seem to be hurting for money, so why was he living with his mother?

None of her business.

"This buckles into the seat…" Mackenzie quickly installed the doggy booster seat in Cade's truck and showed him how to attach her collar to it.

"Thank you for everything, Mackenzie." Christy hugged her. "If you need anything, give us a call. I hope to see a lot more of you. Cade does, too, don't you?" With the back of her hand, she playfully slapped his stomach.

He sighed loudly and gave Mackenzie a tight smile. "We'll let you get settled. If you're not busy tomorrow night, you're welcome to join us at the community center for a Jewel River Legacy Club meeting. It will give you a chance to get to know some of the residents."

"I'd like that."

"It starts at seven."

"Thanks. I'll be there." Mackenzie backed up a few steps and waved to them as they buckled in and drove away.

Good. The meeting would give her the opportunity to get the word out that she was ready to treat large animals. Her trailer was fully equipped to haul to any ranch or farm in the area. As for pets, the clinic's renovations would take a few more weeks before it would be ready to open.

Mackenzie strode between the two buildings where the mobile vet trailer was parked. Working with Dr. Johan up in Montana had been exactly what she'd needed before moving here. She'd gained much-needed experience with cattle and the occasional horse, plus Dr. Johan had helped her order this trailer and all the equipment. She'd driven his mobile vet clinic so often, hauling this one would feel like second nature at this point.

She wasn't sure what the future held, but she knew one thing: whatever troubles she faced would be worth it to live in the same town as her father again. It had been too long since they'd spent time together on a regular basis. She couldn't wait until he moved to Jewel River, too.

Growing up, she'd helped him train and take care of the service dogs. She'd loved the simple dinners with her father. They'd discuss the dogs and their days. She missed her dad more than she cared to admit. That was why she'd taken a leap of faith to move here. Dad had been the one who believed in her enough to encourage her to branch out on her own. And he'd suggested opening the small vet clinic three days a week so she could focus on the mobile vet duties the other two.

He'd also assured her that if working with large animals proved too much for her, she could always focus on pets and hire another vet to round out the practice. It would make life easier for her, but she didn't want to.

It was time to overcome her nerves about treating horses and cattle. It was time to find out what she was really made of.

Chapter Two

Despite the temptation to eavesdrop on his mom's conversation with Mary Corning, Cade focused on the entrance to the community center. He was surprised Mackenzie hadn't arrived yet. The meeting would be starting soon. He wanted to introduce her to some of the members, partly because he felt responsible for convincing her to move to Jewel River and partly to show he was a respected member of the community and not some man-child dependent on his mother.

"…and I told her no way that was going to be enough dessert for an O'Leary family reunion, but she insisted two dozen cookies and a pan of brownies would suffice…" Mary's voice rose as his mother made sympathetic murmurs. "I mean has she looked at her brother lately? John's only a few inches shy of seven feet tall. The man can eat…"

Cade mentally conceded two dozen cookies and a pan of brownies would not be enough for an O'Leary family reunion. Mary was correct about that.

Where was Mackenzie? Had she already gotten called out to a ranch? Yesterday, while they'd loaded Tulip's supplies in the backseat of his truck, Cade had noticed the trailer parked next to the clinic. It looked new. A mobile vet trailer would be a big improvement over the plastic bins of outdated equipment Doc Banks had kept in his ancient Ford. Cade would have to ask Mackenzie about the trailer's features at some point. It would be a good selling point for the clients he was hoping would board their horses with him. He'd been courting Forestline Adventures for the past couple of months but, so far, hadn't gotten a firm commitment from them.

"Just tell her to order lemon bars from Annie's Bakery and make a sheet cake. It will all work out." Mom flourished her hand as Mary mumbled something Cade didn't make out. "Tulip? Oh, yes, our little sweetie is a delight. Follows me everywhere. And Tulip just loves Cade. Mackenzie couldn't have picked out a better dog for us. I am *so* glad she moved here. And Cade is, too, aren't you, Cade?"

He ignored his mother. The door opened, and Mackenzie, with her hair pulled back in a ponytail and wearing jeans and a T-shirt, slipped inside and headed straight to an empty chair at the table across from the one where he sat. Erica Cambridge took her position in the front to speak to everyone sitting at the tables shoved together to form a U.

"Oh, there's Mackenzie now." His mom's voice lowered as she spoke to Mary. "Isn't she a cutie?"

He braced himself for his mother to try to drag him into the conversation. If Mom publicly asked him if he thought she was "a cutie," he would mentally lose it.

Erica clapped her hands to get everyone's attention. Then Clem Buckley, a retired rancher tougher than a two-dollar steak, led everyone in the Pledge of Allegiance and the Lord's Prayer. Erica then went through old business.

"Angela, where are we at with this year's Shakespeare-in-the-Park film?" She addressed Angela Zane, a good-natured woman and one of the livelier members of Jewel River Legacy Club.

"I'm happy to report that after last summer's smashing success of *Romeo and Juliet: Wyoming Style*, Joey had a big uptick in people wanting to take part in *A Jewel River Mid-summer Night's Dream*. He had to bring in an assistant—little Lindsey Parker, Joe and Abby's youngest. She's the one who sprained her ankle trying to do those hurdles at the track meet last year. Wasn't her fault she couldn't clear them. They were set too tall, if you ask me—"

"Yes, we all know Lindsey." Erica had mastered the art of moving along the prone-to-get-sidetracked members during these meetings. Angela's grandson, Joey, was a junior in high school with a talent for creating and editing videos. Whenever he made one related to a club proposal, it tended to add spice to the meetings. Cade, personally, enjoyed all the special effects. "How is she helping Joey?"

"He put Lindsey in charge of auditions, and she's working with him on plot development. Joey wants to really show off our part of Wyoming and give the story a Jewel River feel."

"I'm sure he does," Erica said. "Will everything be ready by mid-August?"

"Oh, yes." Angela nodded with enthusiasm. "Don't you worry, hon, the film will be ready in time. Just like last year."

"Are the characters falling into piles of cow patties in this one, too?" Clem asked loudly. A few titters spread throughout the room.

"I'm not sure. I can ask Joey if you'd like." Angela didn't seem to grasp that Clem was being sarcastic. "I do know they're trying to figure out how to add a herd of pronghorns in one of the scenes, and I believe the strange character—Bottom, is it?—his head might be turned into a moose instead of a donkey. Don't you worry, Joey has a *lot* of special effects up his sleeve."

Cade wasn't surprised at all. Maybe the kid would add a rocket to this one. Who knew?

Erica checked her notes. "Let us know if Joey and Lindsey

need anything from us. The online fundraiser has been set up to cover the costs of costumes, sets and equipment." She then turned to Marc Young, who headed up one of the committees. "Any updates on the empty buildings?"

"The former industrial park still has three for sale..." Marc, a local rancher and one of Cade's good friends, had married Erica's sister, Reagan, a few months ago. Fun wedding. Cade had been one of the groomsmen. Reagan owned and operated a thriving gourmet chocolate store in town. Cade should probably stop in there soon for another box of her dark-chocolate covered caramels. His mouth watered just thinking about them.

Marc nodded toward Mackenzie. "Once Dr. Howard gets settled, her clinic and her father's service-dog training center are sure to bring traffic to the area. I think we can anticipate the other buildings getting new occupants in the near future."

"Good point," Erica said. "By the way, everyone, this is our new veterinarian." She turned her attention to Mackenzie and made a rising motion. "Why don't you stand up and tell us about yourself?"

"Hello, I'm Mackenzie Howard. I grew up in South Dakota, got my undergrad at the University of Wyoming—go Cowboys!—and was accepted into the Doctor of Veterinary Medicine program at Texas A&M. I specialized in rural and mixed animals and have been working for a veterinarian clinic in Cheyenne for the past five years."

"Do you have any experience with cattle?" Clem gave Mackenzie a cool stare.

"Yes, sir, I do. In addition to my residency, I spent the past several months working with a large animal vet up in Montana."

"What about in Cheyenne?" Clem made a sucking sound with his teeth. "What did you do there?"

The question didn't seem to fluster her. "I treated pets. Dogs, cats, the occasional wild animal."

"Hmm." Clem shrugged, appearing lukewarm about her credentials. "Takes a good cowboy years to understand the ins and outs of cattle. A couple of months ain't gonna cut it."

"Clem, will you stop grilling her?" Christy glared razor blades his way. "Mackenzie is more than qualified."

"Grilling?" Clem threw his hands up. "What did I say?"

"It's the way you're saying it. It's disrespectful."

"I just want to know if the doc here knows what she's all about."

"She knows what she's all about." An abundance of attitude came through his mother's words. Great, Mom was getting worked up. When her chin bobbed as she spoke, watch out.

"What I don't know, I'll figure out," Mackenzie said. "As a veterinarian, I feel like I learn something new every day. I suppose I always will." She calmly surveyed the rest of the room. "If any of you have horses or cattle, I can drive out to your property with my fully equipped mobile vet trailer. It's set up and ready for business. My clinic here in town should be ready for pets by the end of the month. It'll be open Mondays, Wednesdays and Fridays to treat cats, dogs and other small animals. I'm in the process of hiring a vet tech, but I still need a part-time receptionist, so if anyone is looking for a job, send them my way."

"What kind of hours are those?" Clem sounded flabbergasted. "You're only working three days a week?"

"They're travel-vet hours." From the way her jaw tightened, Cade guessed Mackenzie's patience was wearing thin. "I often work seven days a week. I'm on call for any emergencies, and I'm leaving Tuesdays and Thursdays free for large-animal care. Like I said, the trailer's ready, so if anyone has cows or horses needing treatment, call me. Oh, I have business cards."

Mackenzie reached down and grabbed the string bag she'd set on the floor. Then she pulled out a small stack of cards and passed them to Johnny Abbot on her right. He took one and passed the stack down.

"We're grateful you're here, Mackenzie," Erica said. "Dr. Banks has been gracious enough to help out with emergencies, but it will be a relief to have regular treatment for our cattle and horses again. Winston Ranch will be using your services."

"I'm glad to hear it." Mackenzie nodded. A shadow passed over her face, making Cade wonder if she had regrets about moving here. Had Clem gotten to her? Or was something else going on that he wasn't aware of?

Erica moved on to the next order of business. Mary Corning admitted her lack of progress on putting together a survey on whether to add a pickleball court to Memorial Park.

"I don't know what questions to put on the survey." Mary opened her hands as her shoulders lifted.

"No one here wants to play pickleball," Clem said. "Why can't you ever suggest something practical?"

"Pickleball *is* practical. My niece in Ohio says it's all the rage there right now. I'm sure a lot of people around here would like to get in on the fun."

"Fun?" Clem said. "Riding horses is fun. Going fishing is fun. Waving a paddle around a court that would fit in a dollhouse is not fun. Why do they call it pickleball, anyhow? Are dills involved?"

"Mary," Erica said loudly to override Clem, "why don't you talk to Janet Reese about setting up an online survey? She's done them before. And we can leave a stack of printouts at the library, too."

"I'll do that." Mary's chin rose. The meeting continued.

Cade updated everyone on his committee's progress on assessing if a workout center in town would be viable. When he finished, he counted the minutes until the meeting ended. As soon as Erica dismissed everyone, he stood, hoping to head off Mackenzie before she left.

"Oh, Mackenzie?" Mom called out so loudly it caused a few people on their way to the door to turn back and look at her. "You should join Cade's committee if you're thinking of becoming a member. You two have so much in common."

"I'm sure she doesn't have time—" Cade stopped in his tracks.

"I don't have time—" Mackenzie, wide-eyed, said.

"Will you stop your matchmaking, woman?" Clem was several feet away from Christy, and it was a good thing. Cade did not want to have to separate those two. He'd also never wanted to disappear as much as he did in this moment. So he responded the way he always did, by making it into a joke.

"Don't worry, Clem." Cade grinned. "I wouldn't be surprised if she was fixing up an online dating app for the singles in Jewel River as we speak."

"I am not—" Mom lifted her fingers in air quotes "—'fixing up an online dating app.' Although now that you mention it, I think it's a fabulous idea. You boys could certainly use it." His mom redirected all her annoyance at Clem, and Cade walked away as Clem scoffed.

"Wouldn't surprise me, you know," Clem said. "Desperate. That's what you are. You're desperate for a wedding."

"I am *not* desperate."

"Instead of worrying about your son's love life," Clem continued, "why don't you take one of those remedial driving courses? Maybe you'd be able to keep your license for more than two weeks at a time and could get yourself some independence."

"Oh, so now I'm desperate *and* dependent? I can drive just fine…" His mother's voice rose.

Cade hurried over to where Mackenzie was stuffing the remaining business cards in her string bag.

"Sorry about things getting a little heated in here. My mom and Clem can be…" He shook his head. He had no words to describe either of them. "Do you want me to introduce you to some of the members?"

She glanced around, and he realized everyone had either left or was on their way out.

"Too late." Her left cheek flashed a dimple, and he couldn't look away from it. She wriggled the bag's strings onto her shoulders. "How's Tulip settling in?"

"Great. For a small thing, she sure has a lot of personality." They both headed to the door. "She made herself right at home. Mom's spoiling her, and she's eating it up."

"Is your mom working with her on the commands we went over?"

"She is and I am, too." He held the door for her and followed her out into the warm night. "Don't worry. My mom loves to spoil kids and pets, but she's no pushover, not even with Tulip."

"That's good to hear."

They stood outside on the sidewalk in awkward silence for a few moments. Several topics came to mind, but he couldn't seem to put them into words. What was it about her that tied his tongue into knots?

She pointed to her truck. "Well, I guess I'll see you next week."

"Yeah." Disappointment settled over him. He didn't want

her to leave. But he couldn't seem to toss out a charming line to make her stay.

Something was definitely wrong with him.

He rocked back on his heels. "You'll be so busy getting calls and driving out to ranches, you might regret our training sessions." That was what he'd come up with? *Real smooth.*

"I hope so. I need those calls. I have a lot invested in this move." She angled her head. "But I won't regret helping you and your mother train Tulip. That little dog is going to brighten a lot of people's lives."

"Yes, she will."

The glance she gave him had questions in it...and doubts.

Why would she doubt him? He stiffened. He wasn't one to brag. Never felt the need to list all of his accomplishments.

But the look she'd thrown his way? Made him want to tell her all about the large, profitable cattle ranch he owned thirty minutes from town. Not to mention the sprawling property on the outskirts of Jewel River where his high-end horse-boarding facility with state-of-the-art stables, riding paths and acres of fenced pastures would be located. Then there was his portfolio of investments, which included several properties right here in Jewel River.

Mackenzie knew none of it. And she didn't need to know, either. He had nothing to prove to her.

"See you on Monday," she said.

"See ya."

She turned and strolled to her truck. She clearly didn't view him as successful and independent. More like a guy joined at the hip to his mommy. Or merely one half of the mother-son team training Tulip.

It was probably better that way.

He hadn't forgotten his past. A down-to-earth woman like Mackenzie would be repulsed by his ethical lapse. If she wasn't impressed with him now, she certainly wouldn't be impressed with the old him—the one still lurking deep inside.

If he could wipe that entire time frame from his memory, he would.

The single life was his penance for his mistakes. But at times like this, he wished he could have more.

"Ah, there's my girl." Two days later on Thursday afternoon, Patrick Howard held his arms open inside the entrance of Mackenzie's clinic.

"Dad!" What a great surprise! After rising from the floor, where she'd been checking out the newly installed cabinets, Mackenzie ran to him and laughed as he hugged her. "I thought you were in Texas all week."

"Finished early." He released her and took in the reception area—still a work in progress. "This is it, huh? It's a good space. The right size. I was worried your building would be too small."

"I was, too, but it's bigger than it looks." She still couldn't get over the fact her dad was here. He looked younger than his sixty-two years. He was in good shape—worked out daily in addition to training the service dogs—and he had on a plain black T-shirt, jeans and boots. She hitched her head to the side. "Come on, I'll show you around."

She took him through all the rooms, noting his comments and suggestions. They ended up in the large back warehouse space.

"I've already had a training session with Christy and Cade. They seem to be a good fit for Tulip."

"Did you tell them your old man taught you everything you know?" His blue eyes twinkled.

"If I didn't, I should have. You really *did* teach me everything I know about dog training."

"You wanted to learn. That's half the battle."

"It looked good on my application to get into the vet program, too."

"It sure didn't hurt." He pointed to the door. "Mind taking a break? I'm itching to check out my building."

"I am, too. I haven't been inside yet. I thought it would be fun to go through it together. Let me grab the keys." She'd been the one to pick up the keys to both buildings from the realtor when she'd arrived in town. It had taken considerable self-control for her to refrain from checking out the large building next to the clinic. Would it be full of junk? Torn up? No matter what shape it was in, her father would find a silver lining somewhere. It was his personality to find the good in things. She, on the other hand, was always preparing herself to be let down.

They emerged into the late-afternoon sunshine. A breeze kept the temperature in the low seventies, perfect in her mind.

"Any calls yet to try out the trailer?" he asked.

"Not yet." Mackenzie was trying not to let it bother her, but she was surprised she hadn't gotten a single call. All last summer, Cade had made it sound as if the veterinarian situation was dire. "I'm sure they'll start calling when they realize I'm open for business. I went to a local meeting Tuesday night to get the word out."

After the meeting, she'd settled on her couch and searched for information about Cade. She'd unearthed an article in a business trade journal about him. He'd graduated from the University of Michigan and immediately had been hired by a global investment bank in New York City. He'd quickly become a star. Been promoted multiple times. The article was from six years ago. She'd found no information since, not even a social-media profile of the man.

Something had happened to bring him back to Jewel River. But what?

"Your phone will be ringing nonstop soon." Her father studied the exterior as they approached the entrance.

Would it? That Clem guy had been awfully confrontational. Were the ranchers around here skeptical of her skills?

Why would they be? She might be on the younger side, but she had good credentials. And she didn't think her gender was an issue. It hadn't been in the past. Still, she'd be the first to admit, she wasn't as experienced with large animals as they might have been hoping for. It didn't make her a complete novice, though.

Dad unlocked the double glass doors, and they entered a small entryway with another set of double glass doors. "This is a nice feature. The entryway will help keep out the cold."

"Good point." She continued inside, and her dad switched on the lights. "Wow."

"You can say that again. I'm glad the previous owner didn't go through with their plan to convert it into a machine shop. The fact it was a warehouse will make it easier for me to lay out the space."

Mackenzie marveled at how wide-open it was. Small windows near the ceiling were spaced apart every ten feet or so, and at the other end, a tall garage door allowed for a bay. To the right, a hallway led to offices and bathrooms.

"I have a feeling this place is going to need extra insulation and a top-notch furnace." Dad strolled to the middle of the warehouse. "And I haven't solved the problem of where the clients are going to stay while they're here learning how to handle their dogs. Obviously, their accommodations need to be accessible to people with disabilities. Have you had a chance to snoop around town much?"

"No, I haven't. Sorry." She'd been so busy trying out the

equipment in the trailer and overseeing the renovations at the clinic that she hadn't ventured out beyond the grocery store and diner. "I can ask Cade for suggestions on Monday."

"Yeah, good plan. Ask him if there's a hotel or old apartments we could fix up for my clients."

"He seems to have the pulse of Jewel River."

"What makes you say that?"

Mackenzie lifted one shoulder, dragging the toe of her canvas sneaker in the dust. Her instincts were usually pretty accurate. "I mean, he sold us this property, and I wouldn't have even considered moving here if it wasn't for him."

"Well, he's a good salesman, I'll give him that."

Mackenzie knew what he was thinking. He'd reserve further comment until he met Cade in person. Her father was a good judge of character. She was curious to find out his take on the man.

Personally, she considered Cade Moulten a little too good to be true.

Too gorgeous. Too involved with the community. Too smart. Too savvy, given his experience in New York finance. Too available to help his mother.

Why was he so generous with his time? Did the guy have a selfish bone in his body? There must be an ulterior motive in there somewhere.

Dad crouched to inspect an electrical outlet. The bundled wires climbed the wall, then edged along the ceiling. "I don't like exposed wires. I'll have to do something about those, too."

"Add it to your list."

"Have you heard from your mother?" Dad straightened to stare at her.

"No." Where had that question come from? "Why?"

"Just wondering. Did you tell her you moved?"

"Why would I do that?"

"I'm sure she'd like to know."

"So she can drive up here and gush about how great I'm doing and then vanish with barely a wave goodbye? No thanks." She hated hearing the bitterness in her tone. She'd been praying to let go of her anger toward her mother, but every time she thought of the woman, her chest tightened and something hard locked around her heart.

"She loves you, Mackenzie."

"She has a funny way of showing it."

"Like I always say, she is who she is."

"And like I always say, it's not my job to care. I don't know why you defend her." She turned away from him, hoping to suppress the adrenaline firing through her veins.

He sighed. "I don't know, either. Maybe I wish you could have known your mom when she was full of energy and ideas. Back when she cared."

"Yeah, well, the full of energy and ideas I remember. Living with her was pure chaos. As for her caring about us? Sorry, you're on your own there."

With sadness in his eyes, he slowly nodded. "You know a good place to eat around here? I'm hungry."

"That I *can* help you with." She grinned. "You're going to love Dixie B's. Huge portions and down-home cooking."

"Now you're talking."

As Mackenzie led the way out of the building, Cade crowded her mind. He had a close relationship with his mother. Where was his dad? Maybe they'd divorced like her own parents had. Maybe his father had passed away… or was she wrong on both counts? He might be around. She didn't think so, though.

The way Christy acted made Mackenzie think she relied on Cade. Strange, since the woman seemed so independent.

The two were together all the time, though. And Christy definitely had matchmaking on her mind.

Mackenzie shivered. She'd hate to break it to the Moultens, but the more Mackenzie was pushed in one direction, the more she dug in her heels to go the other way. Regardless of what Christy hoped for, Mackenzie was not looking for a boyfriend.

Her work already took up most of her life, and something told her getting her practice up and running would take every free minute she had.

She had no time or room in her life for romance. And she planned on keeping it that way.

"I wish I could bring you with me, Tulip. But it will be a few more weeks before you can meet my nana." Cade petted the dog lounging on his lap as he sat on the sectional in the living room Friday afternoon. It had been a typical day. This morning he'd checked cattle with his ranch manager for a few hours, then he'd gotten cleaned up and dropped off Mom at the nursing home. From there, she had plans with friends to do something or another.

After dropping her off, he'd made the five-minute drive to Moulten Stables to check the construction progress. Everything was on track. So why did he have this nagging worry that something would go wrong?

Tulip let out a contented sigh and snuggled deeper into his lap. She'd blended into their household so quickly it was hard to remember what life had been like without her. He shifted, and her little head rose as if to say, *Don't even think about getting up, mister.*

"I know, I know. It's naptime. When isn't it, though?" He chuckled to himself. He enjoyed the feel of her soft fur. "We'll hang out when I get back."

Every evening, he and his mother had been taking her on a stroll around the property to get her used to walking loosely beside them. Tulip seemed to love the walks. She'd sniff around the trees and trot beside them with her head held high.

"I really do need to go." Cade picked up Tulip as he stood. Cradling her to his chest, he smiled at her. "Soon, you'll get to come with me and sit on Nana's lap. She loves dogs."

Tulip licked his hand, and he laughed.

A few minutes later, he got into his truck. He texted Ty before starting it up. I'm on my way to Nana's.

His brother's response came right away. Leaving now.

As soon as Cade arrived at the nursing home, he got out of his truck. Ty came over, and Cade pulled him into a half hug, then hitched his thumb toward the entrance. "You ready for this?"

"As ready as I'll ever be." Two years younger than him, Ty always seemed to have the weight of the world on his shoulders. Spontaneous smiles were rare occurrences, and as much as Cade and Mom hoped time would heal his wounds, Ty was as reclusive as he'd been when Zoey passed away.

He missed his brother. Wanted the old Ty back. But he'd take this version of him over the one who wouldn't leave his house. Any progress was better than none. It was one of the reasons he insisted Ty visit their grandmother with him every Friday afternoon. Got him out and about.

"Let's catch up a minute first."

Ty was physically similar to him but on the leaner side. Their personalities were where they differed. Cade was outgoing, where Ty was reserved. After Dad died, Cade had quickly realized he wasn't suited to full-time ranching, so he'd hired an experienced manager to take care of the cattle. Ty, on the other hand, was happiest riding horseback around his ranch every day, preferably alone.

They each had their own land and their own cattle operations thanks to their father's business decisions. After Cade went away to college, Dad had split the massive ranch into two and continued to run half while Ty took over the other part. They'd all agreed if Cade changed his mind about his career, he'd take over their father's portion. If he didn't, Ty would run both. Their father's death had made that decision for Cade. He'd moved back to Wyoming permanently a week after the funeral.

"Do you think she'll recognize us this time?" Ty asked.

"She did last week. I'm hoping these visits will be easier when Tulip can come with us."

"Yeah, she'll like having a dog to pet." Ty swatted away a fly. "Remember Skippy?"

"How could I forget? Droopiest eyes on a hound I've ever seen."

"How's the training going? Mom not so subtly suggested I get to know Mackenzie better, and I told her I would block her number if she mentioned it again."

"Is that how you get her off your back? I wish I could do that. It's a little harder when you live with her."

Ty's eyebrows rose as if to say *don't I know it*. Over the years, Cade had learned there was nothing he could do to prevent his mother's schemes to get daughters-in-law and, eventually, grandkids. He simply threw himself into his work and ignored her.

"How are the stables coming along?"

"Great. They're framing the stalls next week. I reached out to the companies hosting outdoor retreats around the state. Forestline Adventures might be interested in wintering their horses here."

"Are they the ones with all the luxury rentals?"

"Yeah, they organize hunting and fishing trips from first

thaw to mid-October. Expensive trips. They need reliable, healthy horses for their clients, and rumor has it they're tired of the hassle of taking care of the horses all winter. I guess they've been struggling to find good help, and they lost two horses to injury and illness last year."

"That's where you come in." Was that a hint of a smile on Ty's face? Oh, to see a full smile again. Cade tried not to be greedy, but his brother meant the world to him. *God, please bring my brother back. He deserves to be happy. Unlike me.*

"Yes. I can board all their current horses and rent them any additional horses they might need in the summer."

"Sounds like a win-win for you both."

"Yeah, but I have a feeling they're going to want a veterinarian on call specifically certified for horses."

Ty let out a snort. "They aren't going to find any of those around here. Near Jackson Hole, maybe."

"Yeah." He hadn't brought up the veterinarian situation to them, but before he could present them with a contract, it would need to be addressed. He'd already waited to begin construction on the stables until Mackenzie and her father had bought his buildings. He'd needed to be certain there would be a vet in the area before moving forward with his plans.

And now he couldn't stop wondering if having a vet was enough.

He needed the right vet.

What was the point in going through the expense of developing the property if he couldn't be certain it would be profitable?

It never stopped you before. You were born taking risks.

And look where it had gotten him.

"If you're worried," Ty said, "why don't you talk to them about it? Now that we have a vet practicing in town, they should be fine."

But that was where his brother was wrong. Ty didn't know how life outside of this small town worked, and Cade did. He understood how the elite thought and lived—he'd been one of them for years.

Companies like Forestline Adventures catered to extremely wealthy business people. Everything had to be the best, including the horses, the stables, the facilities and even the veterinarian treating the horses. All of it wrapped around status.

"I'll figure it out." Cade clapped his hand on Ty's shoulder. "Let's go see Nana."

They strode together to the glass doors leading into the brick one-story building. Red, purple and white flowers waved a cheery greeting. Inside the building, Charlene Parker, one of his mother's best friends, raised her hand in greeting from the reception desk. In her late fifties, she wore scrubs and had a big smile. Her daughter, Janey, had gotten engaged to Lars Denton at Christmas, and Charlene liked to give Cade all the updates on the upcoming wedding, whether he wanted them or not. He wasn't into weddings and all that, but it made her happy to tell him, and it didn't cost him a thing to listen.

"Howdy, boys, Miss Trudy is in good spirits today."

That was a relief. "Thanks, Charlene. How've you been?"

"Good, hon. Janey had a hiccup with the florist. We're trying to figure out the bouquets. Your mother has been my rock. I don't know what I'd do without her."

"If you want to borrow her, give me a holler. Keep her at your place for a while. A month. Two. More." He always teased about his mother. Charlene ate it up.

"Oh, you!" She waved him off and laughed. "I have to tell you I do agree with her on one thing—it's a crime that you two strapping cowboys are single. If my Janey was still on the market, you can guarantee I'd want her to snatch up one of you boys."

"It's a shame she's taken." Cade grinned. He glanced at Ty. His brother looked positively green. "We'd better get in there."

As they made their way down the hallway, Ty gave him a sideways glance. "That's why I stay home."

"She doesn't mean anything by it." Cade focused on the wreath his mom had hung on Nana's door up ahead.

"Are you sure about that?" Ty sounded a little disgusted and slightly terrified. "No one is *snatching* me up. I'm done with women."

Cade knew better than to argue when Ty was about to launch into one of his *I'm done with women* rants. Next would be a lament about how he'd had the only woman he'd ever loved, and God had taken her from him, and he'd never love again. Cade didn't blame him, but the familiar words did get stale after a while.

Cade stopped at the open door and knocked twice before entering. "Hi, Nana."

Sitting in her wheelchair, she turned and smiled at them. "Cade! Did you bring Ty today?"

"I'm here, Nana." Ty removed his cowboy hat. They took turns bending to hug her, then they each sat in a chair to visit for a while.

The room was nice enough. She didn't have to share it with anyone, and his mom had added plants and some of Nana's favorite pictures from home. His mother also decorated the bulletin board every month with a new theme. At the moment, it had a purple and yellow border and pictures of pansies and kittens on it.

"How are you feeling today?" Cade asked.

"As good as can be." Her cloudy blue eyes brightened.

"We had chocolate ice cream and listened to a man play guitar."

Every afternoon, the nursing home had activities for any of the residents who wanted to participate.

"What kind of music?" Ty asked.

"All kinds. I clapped along, but I sure would have liked to dance. Your grandfather was a fine dancer. He'd twirl me around like I weighed less than a feather."

He and Ty laughed. "You probably did." She'd always been a bitty thing.

"Your mother said there will be a little dog coming soon."

"Yes, her name's Tulip. She has some more training to complete before we can bring her."

Nana clasped her hands to her chest. Her eyes looked suspiciously watery. "I can't wait. I love dogs. It will be so nice to pet one again."

Cade's heart tugged. The woman missed her husband, couldn't dance and was confined to either her bed or the wheelchair. All she really looked forward to was the chance to pet a dog. Maybe if he and Mom worked extra hard with Tulip, they could speed up the process.

He wanted Nana to have something to look forward to. Before it was too late. "We'll bring her as soon as we can."

After twenty minutes, they hugged Nana once more and left.

"That wasn't too bad." Ty strode beside him down the hall.

"Wish every visit went that well." Cade didn't stop at the reception desk since Charlene wasn't around. They turned the corner and headed out the doors.

"Do you think Tulip will help her?"

"I don't know. If nothing else, it will make her happy. I'd train five dogs if I thought it would slow her dementia, but at the end of the day, there's nothing we can do about it."

They emerged into the sunshine and continued through the parking lot until they reached their trucks.

"I'm sick and tired of losing people I love." Ty balled his hands into fists.

"I know." Cade blew out a frustrated breath. "I'll do what I can with Tulip."

Ty ducked his chin, shaking his head. "It won't matter. Nothing will help."

"I guess all we can do is make the best of the time we have with her."

Ty exhaled loudly. "I'm taking off."

"We could get a pizza. Hang out."

"Another time."

Cade figured Ty would say that, but it made him feel bad just the same. "All right. See you later."

Mackenzie had said Tulip's training shouldn't take more than six weeks. So why did he feel like he was running out of time? The sooner the dog was ready to visit Nana, the better.

Chapter Three

Had Cade brought her to Jewel River under false pretenses?

The following Monday, Mackenzie showed Christy and Cade the commands for Tulip to lie down and stay. They were blessed Tulip was such an eager little dog. Well, that and the fact Mackenzie had already taught her several commands when the dog was living with her. Their session was about to wrap up, and when it did, she needed to pull Cade aside and have a tough conversation with him.

It had been almost a week since the Legacy Club meeting, and she'd gotten exactly zero calls from ranchers or horse owners. No one seemed to be desperate for her services. In fact, no one seemed to want her services at all.

That was not what Cade had told her so many times on the phone.

"I think that should do it for tonight." Mackenzie bent to give Tulip one more treat before petting her fluffy head. "She's a fast learner. In a few weeks, I'll bring in a wheelchair, and we'll train her how to handle being around it."

"Will we be able to take her to the nursing home after that?" The intensity in Cade's eyes confused her. He must really be into training Tulip. Or did he have unrealistic expectations about Tulip helping his grandmother?

"No, she needs to be certified. But we'll go on a field trip first to teach Tulip how to respond to the nurses, residents and all the new scents and sounds she'll be dealing with. I'll clear it with the director."

"Nana is so excited to meet Tulip." Christy squeezed Cade's biceps, then took the leash from him. "It's going to make her day when we bring this little princess in for the first time."

Mackenzie wished her dad could have stayed in town one more day to meet Christy and Cade, but he'd left yesterday afternoon to head back to the training center he worked for. Two more weeks. Then he'd officially be self-employed. Here in Jewel River. She couldn't wait.

"Christy, why don't you practice with Tulip for a bit. I need to discuss something with Cade."

Her eyes grew round as she nodded rapidly. "Take your time. I'll be fine right here with our girl. No rush. You two get to know each other better."

"Seriously, Ma?" Cade's frustrated eye roll and the way he was shaking his head would have made Mackenzie chuckle if she wasn't so keyed up.

"What?" His mom's innocent protest didn't fool either of them.

"Never mind," he muttered.

Mackenzie led the way through the door to the main clinic. The contractor she'd hired had finished most of the work. The cabinets and counters had been installed in the reception area. All new waterproof flooring had been put in throughout the space. The kennel room and bathrooms were completed, too. The only thing left to finish was installing the equipment in the surgery room. Once that was done, she'd be able to get the final permit, and Jewel River Veterinary Services would be ready to open.

When she entered her office, Mackenzie whirled around

to face Cade. He stood in the doorway with a confused look on his face.

"Were you being completely honest with me?" she asked.

His cheeks slackened, then his eyebrows drew together. "About what?"

"About how much this area needs a vet." She crossed her arms over her chest and felt her jaw lock. She tried to relax it and failed.

"Of course, why?" Faint color flushed his cheeks.

"Because I haven't gotten a single call from anyone needing my services."

"Really?" He shifted his weight to one hip and seemed to consider it. "I wonder why."

"Yeah, I wonder why, too." The words flew out with an edge. "Is there something going on I should know about?"

"Not that I'm aware of."

They stood in tense silence.

"You handed out your business cards at the meeting." He seemed to be talking to himself. "Several ranchers attended, so they should have your number. Do you have a website set up?"

The website. She mentally cringed. She'd started putting together a DIY site, but it wasn't finished. She needed to make the website a priority. "Not yet."

"Let me see one of the cards." He held out his hand. She went behind the desk and rummaged through a box of supplies until she found one. Then she straightened and handed it to him. He read it and gave it back. "It's the right number, correct?"

She hadn't thought of that. What if she'd accidentally had them printed with the wrong number? The thought was so horrifying, she didn't even want to look. But she did. And to her relief, her cell number was correct.

"It's the right number."

"Then I'm not sure what to tell you. Unless… I mean…it's summer. Not everyone has a need for a vet right now. That will change in a few months with preg checks. Plus, a lot of people in the surrounding area don't even know you're here. I suppose it will take some time for the word to get out."

She didn't have time. She'd sunk a lot of cash into this venture, and she had living expenses to pay for.

Shaking her head, she tried to think of what could have gone wrong. Maybe she was being impatient. Cade was right. Not many people were aware she'd opened a practice here. And until the clinic opened, they might not know. If she was being honest with herself, the bulk of her income would be from treating pets in the clinic, anyhow.

Cade wasn't the enemy. Why had she automatically blamed him for her problems?

Because you're used to Mom convincing you to help her, then feeling like a fool when you realize she manipulated you for her own reasons. And now you've thrown Cade into the same category. Good job.

"Hey, I know this can feel overwhelming." He bent his head slightly to gaze into her eyes. A flutter rippled across her skin at the kindness in his stare. "It will all fall into place. You've gotten a lot done already. I can't believe how quickly this clinic came together. And the trailer looks amazing. I wouldn't mind taking a tour of it sometime when you get a chance."

"Really?" No one besides her dad had shown the slightest interest in the trailer…or in her. Okay, that wasn't true. Yesterday, a few older women had stopped by her rental house in town to drop off cookies and introduce themselves. They'd been nice. Nosy, but nice.

Cade wasn't the enemy. He'd been on her side from day one.

"Do you want to see the trailer now?" she asked.

A grin spread across his face, and he nodded. "Sure, why not?"

"Come on. I'll give you the tour."

Why was Mackenzie questioning his integrity? Did she really think so little of him—that he would lie to get her to move here?

Was there a grain of truth in it, though? One of the reasons he'd pushed her to relocate was for his stables. Was he selfish? He wanted her to think he was a stand-up guy.

She clearly didn't.

And deep down he wasn't.

When he'd worked in the city, he'd justified what he'd done for the investment bank. They'd hired him because of his gift for finding more efficient ways to do things. He could locate loopholes where other people wouldn't even think to look. And when he'd been asked to work on one of their special teams, he'd jumped at the chance. Everything had been legal. His bosses and the lawyers they employed—the best in the business—had assured him it was all aboveboard.

But just because something was legal, didn't make it right.

Maybe Mackenzie saw right through him. In some ways, it would be a relief. It would force him to maintain a friendly distance. He'd show up for Tulip's training sessions. Say a brief hello to her if he bumped into her around town. And that was it. It would zap this growing attraction he had for her.

Besides, he was a busy man. Had his hands in a lot of ventures. There was no need for him to feel responsible for Mackenzie's success or lack thereof.

Friendly distance…

They went to the back room, where Mom was practicing commands with Tulip.

"Done already?" Mom asked. "Look, she's a pro at this. Tulip, down." The little dog lay down and rested her chin on her forearms while watching his mom expectantly. "Release. Good girl."

Tulip trotted over and cheerfully accepted her treat.

"I'm going to check out the mobile vet trailer." Cade pointed to the side door. "Mind giving me a few more minutes?"

"Take all the time in the world." His mom beamed. Then she scooped up Tulip and started talking to her in a baby voice. "We'll hang out here, won't we, princess?"

"You ready?" Mackenzie arched her eyebrows at him.

He nodded. They went out the side door and crossed the narrow strip of blacktop between the buildings where she'd parked her trailer. She pulled the key out of her pocket and unlocked the back.

"Here, let me." He pulled up on the handle and swung it open. At the sight of the chute, he whistled. "Wow. This is something."

"Something good, I hope." Mackenzie set one foot on the ledge and hauled herself up. Then she held out her hand. He almost laughed. Didn't really need a boost inside, but he took her hand anyway. Liked the way it felt in his. So much for keeping a friendly distance.

"More than good." The interior had tight quarters. Mackenzie moved along the side of the wall lined with cabinets while he poked around the equipment. "You can do just about everything in here."

"Preg checks, feet trimming, bull testing, mobile X-rays, ultrasounds. I might look into embryos—flushing and freezing—in the future, but I don't have the qualifications yet. I can basically provide health for the whole herd from this trailer."

"It's impressive." He rubbed his thumb and forefinger along his chin. "How do you trim feet? I don't see a belly band."

"Portable hydraulic tilt." She placed her hand on the chute. "I bought the quietest model I could afford."

"Keeps them from getting spooked."

"Exactly." Mackenzie opened the cabinets and showed him the supplies she stored inside. They chatted about vaccinating, checking bulls and some of the common diseases cattle were prone to get in the summer. Then they returned to the blacktop. Anticipation built as he thought of all the possibilities this trailer could bring to the area.

"I'm opening a horse-boarding facility this fall." He adjusted his cowboy hat.

"Yes, you mentioned it."

He had, hadn't he. "I'm wondering if you'd come out sometime. Check out the stables. They're still being built."

"Why?" Her eyes narrowed.

"Do you like horses? I mean, are you a rider?"

"I do like riding. Haven't been on a horse in a decade, though." She closed the trailer's back door and locked it.

"A decade? Why so long?"

"Veterinary school was pretty intense. I had no time, and I never owned a horse, either."

"You rode friends' horses."

She nodded.

"And after you graduated?" He watched her closely, enjoying how open her expressions were. She was honest. Easy to read. Except…a cloud passed over her eyes before she met his gaze.

"It wasn't on my radar. I was busy establishing myself in Cheyenne. I was on call a lot. Didn't leave much time for long horseback rides."

Cade straightened slightly. There was more to it. Her hesitation told him so. He'd always been able to read people and situations. He used this to his advantage more often than not.

"And now?" he asked.

"I don't anticipate having much time for long rides on horseback here, either." She rested her hand on the side of the trailer. "I'll still be on call."

"If you did have time, would you want to ride?" Why was he pressing this?

It probably had something to do with those hooded eyes and her no-nonsense demeanor. It had been ages since he'd been interested in a woman. And no matter how hard he tried to tell his brain he wasn't interested in her, it wasn't listening.

Her eyelashes fluttered, then she stared at her feet. A beat passed. Two. She met his gaze again, and this time she looked vulnerable.

"Yeah, I would." Her voice was soft, softer than he thought possible coming from her. "I've always wanted my own horse. Silly, I suppose. I don't have time to take care of one, and I'd hate to own a horse and neglect it."

"I can't imagine you neglecting an animal." He spoke the truth. She'd devoted her entire life to animal care.

"Yeah, well, a cat or a dog is one thing. But a horse? They need more than I can give at the moment. It's probably why I'm single and can't imagine a husband or kids in my life, either. I can only fit in so much, you know?"

The words were so unexpected, he blinked. The masculine side of him responded to the challenge. Sure, she might not be able to fit *other* guys into her life. But she could fit Cade in. If she really wanted to.

Did he want her to?

No. Friendly distance, remember?

"Of course, my logic doesn't add up until I get some clients here." The wry way the corner of her lips lifted brought on a twinge of guilt.

He wanted her to have those clients. Wanted her to succeed. After all, he was the one who'd convinced her to move here. He was the one who'd spelled out how much they needed a vet.

Not ten minutes ago, she'd basically accused him of lying to her. The last time he'd been called out like that had been in New York City, by his father. Only back then, Dad had been right.

Mackenzie was wrong. He hadn't lied to her. Jewel River did need a veterinarian.

"I tell you what." He hooked a thumb in his pocket. "Why don't you and I drive out to a few of the ranches. Bring your trailer. I'll introduce you, and you can show them what you're all about."

Her expression told him she wasn't keen on the plan. What about him bothered her so much? No one else around here seemed to have an issue with him. In fact, he could have a date any night of the week if he wanted one—but he didn't want one.

He stared at the trailer. "They'll check out your equipment, talk to you in person and see for themselves you know what you're doing."

"I suppose." Her lips tugged down as if she was nauseous.

"Okay, it's not your thing. That's fine." He brought his hands near his chest and stepped back. "I just think it would help if ranchers could see for themselves all you can do for their herds."

"Why are you offering?" Her eyelids formed slits.

"Because you're needed here. For months, I searched for a vet, and now that you've arrived, our animals will get the care they deserve. The sooner you're established, the better off everyone will be." He gave her a lazy grin. "Plus, I need you to be on call for my stables. But you already knew that."

She let out a half snort, half laugh. "You may have mentioned it a time or two."

"So? What do you say?"

"I've got nothing to lose at this point." She shrugged. "Let's do it."

Victory coursed through his veins, and it wasn't lost on him that this type of victory came with a fair amount of trouble.

He had no business spending time with Mackenzie. Not when he was attracted to her. Not when she presented a challenge his personality couldn't seem to turn down. And not when he had zero intention of letting her know the truth about the lines he'd crossed in New York.

He'd introduce her to the local ranchers, and then his duty would be done. But something told him it wouldn't be that easy. Life never was.

Chapter Four

"You don't waste time, do you?" Two days later, Mackenzie finished hooking the trailer to the hitch on her truck, double-checked that it was secure and took a step back. Sunshine beamed down, and the temperature was sure to reach into the high eighties later. Cade stood on the other side of the hitch but, to his credit, didn't try to help. He merely watched her with a twinkle in his eyes.

"I don't. The best time is now, in my opinion." He crooked a finger toward the hitch. "By the way, you're good at that."

"Yeah, well, I've had a lot of practice over the past months." She mentally reviewed that she did indeed have everything needed for their trip to Triple B Ranch. The trailer was fully stocked, and earlier, she'd tossed a few bottles of water and snacks in the backpack she carried instead of a purse. "Are you riding with me? Or do you want me to follow you?"

"We can ride together." He promptly opened the passenger door to her truck and made himself comfortable.

There went her hope of calming her nerves by rehearsing her spiel during the ride. Small talk with Cade wasn't the scenario she'd hoped for, but she couldn't say she was surprised, either. It wouldn't make sense for them to drive separately on a long trip like this.

She climbed into the driver's seat. When Cade had called

her yesterday to tell her he'd arranged for her to meet Marvin Blythe at Triple B Ranch this morning, she'd been taken aback. He didn't mess around when it came to fulfilling his word. While she was grateful he'd arranged the visit, she resented it a little, too.

It would be nice if the ranchers contacted her instead of her having to rely on Cade for an introduction. Oh, well. She didn't have many other options at the moment. Besides, this would give her a chance to start off on the right foot with Mr. Blythe. She hoped he'd call her for more than just emergencies, though. Ideally, she'd take an active role in the health of his herd by coming out on a regular basis for vaccines and checkups.

She started the truck and glanced at Cade. "You'll have to tell me where to go."

"I can do that." His grin caught her off guard. The man was too handsome. "Go to Center Street and take a left. The ranch is close to the county line, so it will take a while to get there. And if you have time in the next week or two, I'd like for you to come out to my place. I've told Micky, my ranch manager, to set some time aside to discuss a plan for our cattle with you."

"Really?" She wasn't surprised Cade would want her services, but it still made her happy. "Tell him I'll come over first thing tomorrow morning."

"I'll text him now."

Mackenzie didn't speak until she'd checked the rearview to verify the trailer was still connected. Once they were on Center Street, she began to relax. The blue sky was full of puffy clouds, and soon they were surrounded by rolling prairie.

"I could get used to this." Cade leaned back with an air of satisfaction.

"Used to what?"

"Having someone else drive for a change."

"Really?" She sent a sideways glance his way. He looked as appealing as ever. His large frame fit well in the truck. Gave his long legs ample room to stretch. The cowboy hat and boots had already won her over. She wished they hadn't.

There was something about a cowboy.

"I'm my mother's chauffer," he said.

"I noticed you're with your mom a lot."

He shifted, arching his brows, but the shimmer in his eyes assured her he wasn't offended. "There's a reason for that. She's...um...how do I put it?" He brought his index finger to his lips. "A terrible driver."

Mackenzie laughed. It wasn't what she'd expected to hear.

"If she's not speeding, she's driving up on the sidewalk in an effort to park, hitting traffic cones or making her own rules about traffic lights. Honestly, I feel safer—and the entire community does, too—when her license gets suspended."

"Christy? A bad driver?" Mackenzie shook her head. "I don't believe it."

"That's because you haven't seen it. Just wait. In two months, she'll be allowed to drive again, and then...well... you've been warned."

"I think you're being melodramatic." She barely noticed the grazing cattle in the distance. The conversation was too much fun.

"I'm being proactive. Honestly, if there was an award for good citizenship in Jewel River, I would win it every year simply for keeping Mom off the streets."

"Um, that phrase didn't come out right." She flashed him an exaggerated grimace.

"Oh!" He chuckled. "Let me rephrase that. For driving Mom around."

"A good citizenship award, huh? You should take it up with the Legacy Club."

"You know, that's a good idea. I might." Cade pointed to the right. "You're going to turn up ahead."

Mackenzie made the turn, and her heart lightened at the sight of the bluish-purple mountains in the distance. "This is beautiful. So empty and wide-open. Have you always lived here, aside from college and…" She didn't mention New York. Didn't want him thinking she'd been stalking him online.

"I grew up here. Moved to Michigan for college. Then New York City after graduation." The words tumbled out quickly, and she got the impression he didn't want to talk about it. Normally, he wasn't one to rush his speech. "After my dad died, I moved back. Can't imagine living anywhere else."

His father *had* passed away. How sad. "How did he die?"

"Cancer. It was aggressive. He'd barely been diagnosed, and he was gone."

"I'm sorry. That must have been hard."

"It was. It's been six years. I still miss him. Mom and Ty do, too."

"Ty is your brother?"

"Yep. He has his own ranch nearby."

"I see. So, in addition to running a cattle ranch, you're opening a horse-boarding facility."

"That's right."

"Then how do you have time to drive out here with me today?" She hoped she didn't sound judgmental or mean, but really, how did he have the time?

"I don't have the patience to manage the ranch on a daily basis. Micky and the ranch hands take care of it. Soon, I'll hire someone to manage Moulten Stables, too. I do keep track of my investment properties and still manage an investment portfolio. I'm never bored."

"Still? Is that what you did in New York City?"

"Not exactly. I started out as a trader in securities finance."

"Started? After that, what did you do?"

"Whatever my employers asked me to do." He turned away to stare out his window, and Mackenzie got the impression the topic was closed.

She couldn't resist asking one more question. "Do you miss it?"

"The job?" He shifted to face her again. "Parts of it. My mind is always on the fast-track. Even now. The accelerated aspect of Wall Street—the split-second decisions—I thrived on that. And I liked living in the city. It's busy. I never had to slow down."

"Didn't you ever want to slow down?" She could relate. Somewhat. She might not have lived in the big city, but her job forced her to be ready for anything at any time.

"Back then, no. Even now, I struggle with it. But I'm trying to learn how to slow down. Not sure I'll ever master it. What about you? You're busy, too. Does it ever bother you?"

"That's a tough question." She thought back over the past decade. "I think it's normal for me at this point. I've been on a time crunch since I graduated from high school. I was always working toward a goal, though, so it didn't bother me."

"Does it now?"

"No. This is what I want. This is what I signed up for. Long, odd hours come with the job."

"That's fair." He nodded more to himself than to her. "Your ideal day—one with no work, no meetings, no errands or appointments—how would you spend it?"

Innocent enough question, but why did it feel so intimate? She tapped her thumbs on the steering wheel. The scenario spread out before her. It should be easy to answer. But her mind was a complete blank.

"I have no idea." She gave him her best *sorry* expression. "What would yours look like?"

"Come on, there must be something you'd want to do if you had time on your hands."

The first thing that flashed through her mind was a memory of riding a horse with her friend Tawny in high school. She could still feel the sun on her face, the breeze blowing through her hair and the relaxing sway of the horse under the saddle.

"I'd probably borrow a horse and go riding. Pack a lunch. Soak in the nature around me." Once the idea formed, she realized she wanted to make it happen—when things were more settled. "What about you?"

"You miss riding horses." He wore a smug smile, and it didn't bother her one bit. "I can help with that, you know."

"I know," she said in an exaggerated manner. "You're building a barn for stables. Opening a horse-boarding facility. You need me to be on call. Trust me, I got the message."

"Good." They rode in easy silence for several miles. Mackenzie kept waiting for him to tell her what he'd do if he had a day off from everything. But he didn't add to the conversation. He made no effort to speak at all.

"You're avoiding my question," she said.

"What question is that?"

"Free time. An entire day. What would you do with it?"

"I'm not much for free time."

They were similar there. Beyond errands and chores, she had few hobbies. Few? Scratch that. None. Did reading veterinary journals count? Her dad was always trying to get her to have a social life.

"I'd probably round up my buddies for some outdoor fun."

"What if you *had* to spend the day alone?"

He cringed. "I thought this imaginary day was supposed to be something I looked forward to? It's starting to feel like a punishment."

"You don't like being by yourself?"

"I didn't say that. And if you're thinking I live with my mother because I'm scared of being alone, you're wrong."

"Why do you live with her?"

"Convenience. It's home. If she could keep her license for more than a month, maybe things would be different. I don't know. I don't like to worry about her."

This guy is actually sweet. Before she could overthink the unexpected tenderness his words brought on, Cade instructed her to turn again, and before long, the truck was kicking up dust down the long drive of Triple B Ranch. Mackenzie parked near the outbuildings and joined Cade as they strolled toward the largest pole barn.

"His office is this way." Cade had barely finished speaking when a burly older gentleman came out of the barn and strode toward them. Everything about him screamed rancher. The hat, the boots, the jeans, the vest, even the mustache.

"Good to see you, Marv." Cade shook the man's hand. "Thanks for agreeing to meet us. This is Mackenzie Howard, the vet I told you about."

"Doc." He shook her hand, but there was a wariness in his expression that gave her pause.

"This is quite the operation you're running, Mr. Blythe."

"Call me, Marv. Everyone does." His chest puffed up. "I raise a lot of cattle. Keeps me on my toes."

She figured she could start by feeling him out on his preferences for their nutritional balance. "May I ask what you're feeding them?"

"What do you think I'm feeding them?" He gave her a disapproving look. "It's summer. They're grazing."

"Of course. I just thought you might want to discuss their nutritional needs."

"I know their nutritional needs. I've been running this ranch for over fifty years."

She was handling this all wrong. And it was extra embarrassing with Cade standing there witnessing it.

"Why don't I show you my mobile vet trailer? Then you can see what I have to offer your cattle and horses. Oh, and pets. I'm guessing you have some herding dogs about."

"That I do." He seemed to calm down at the mention of dogs. "Sometimes I think I've got more dogs than cattle. The missus can't say no to a puppy."

"My father can't either." She chuckled. "He loves dogs. Trains them to be service dogs—that's his job."

"Really?" Marv began walking toward the back of the trailer. "We have two basset hounds, an Australian shepherd, three mini dachshunds—they are spunky little things—a yellow Lab, a black Lab and a Chihuahua. The Chihuahua does not like me. Loves the missus, though. I call it the rat. Then my wife gets mad and chews me out." Grinning, he shook his head as if it couldn't be helped.

For the next half hour, Mackenzie showed him her equipment and explained the general health checks she offered, all while emphasizing the importance of herd health. He asked her about her experience and tried to trip her up with a few scenarios, but she explained how she would handle the situations, and he seemed to accept that she was qualified.

After she locked the trailer, she shook his hand once more. "Thanks again, Marv. Give me a call with any questions or if you need me to come out for anything. I'd be happy to give the dogs their checkups while I'm here, too."

He rubbed his chin, tilting his head to the side. "That might be a good idea. With Doc Banks retiring, it's been a struggle to get them up-to-date on their shots."

"I understand," she said. "Before I come out next time, we can figure out what shots the dogs need, and I'll do a wellness check on them, too."

"Sounds good."

After saying goodbye, Mackenzie and Cade got back into her truck and began the long ride home.

Even with her gaze on the road, she could feel Cade watching her. What was he thinking?

"That went well," he said.

"It could have gone better." She wished she could have worked out a schedule with Marv to come out regularly to check the cattle. All in due time, she supposed.

"Why do you say that?"

"He wasn't exactly enthusiastic about having me come out to care for the cattle."

"He'll call you."

"Maybe."

"When you told him you'd look at the dogs, his demeanor changed. I give it less than two months, and you'll be on a regular schedule with the dogs *and* the cattle."

"I hope you're right." She sighed. "By the way, I finished the website. I stayed up late last night adding pictures and content."

"That's great. Now everyone will know you're available to service the area."

"But will anyone actually want my services?"

"They won't have a choice." He grinned. "You're all they've got."

"Yeah, well, I'm used to being a consolation prize." As soon as the words left her mouth, she wanted to draw them back in. Cade didn't say anything, but the look in his eyes told her he was puzzling through the words to make sense of them.

Whether he did or not didn't really matter. He was right. In time, she'd gain the trust of the local ranchers. She'd make sure of it.

Why would Mackenzie believe she was a consolation prize? The following evening, Cade was still contemplating what she'd said on the ride home yesterday. Why was she on his mind so much? He shouldn't be thinking about her at all.

With long strides, he headed down the final stretch of path that led from the outbuildings to the rear of the ranch house. After letting himself through the back door of the garage, he washed his hands in the mudroom. Voices carried. Female voices.

His mother must have invited friends over. Charlene? Mary? He forced his feet forward, plastered on a smile and hoped to say just a few words before making a quick escape.

"Thank you so much for coming over, Mackenzie."

Mackenzie? Cade halted. Why was she here?

"Tulip seems fine now," Mom said. "I don't know what got into her earlier. You're staying for supper, of course."

"Oh, um, I'd better not."

Cade held his breath. On the one hand, he wanted Mackenzie to leave. Needed some distance between them. The woman had already taken up too many of his thoughts. On the other hand, he wanted to know more about her. Craved being around her.

Either way, hiding was stupid.

He forced his feet forward through the large kitchen into the open living room. Hardwood floors had been installed throughout the house, and his mother had picked out large area rugs to *make the rooms cozier*—her words, not his.

Vaulted ceilings soared above wooden beams. A stacked-stone fireplace climbed one wall. Large windows overlooked the covered front porch and yard.

Mackenzie sat kitty-corner to his mother on the massive gray sectional. Tulip was sleeping on Mackenzie's lap.

"Hey, there." Cade took a seat at the other end of the sectional.

"You're home early." Mom's wide smile amplified the sparkles of delight in her eyes. "I was just telling Mackenzie she needs to have supper with us."

Mackenzie's cheeks grew rosy.

"That's a great idea." Why had he said that? Probably because every time he caught sight of her pretty face and dark blue eyes, he wanted to prolong their time together. He turned to his mom. "Am I grilling tonight?"

"Chicken and shrimp kebabs. They're on skewers in the fridge." Mom turned back to Mackenzie. "I always make extra in case Ty stops by. Have you met my youngest son?"

He frowned. Mom wasn't trying to push Ty and Mackenzie together, was she? He didn't like that thought. Ty was still grieving. And Mackenzie was—

"I haven't," she said. "But I'm hoping to stop by his ranch soon. I understand it borders yours."

"It does. Used to be all one big ranch, but Pete wanted both boys to have their own cattle. Ty's about your age, I'm guessing. Thirty-three."

"I'm thirty-two." Mackenzie absentmindedly petted Tulip, who let out a contented sigh, licked her tiny lips and settled more deeply on her lap.

"Right. I thought so. Anyway, the two of you have a lot in common."

Cade bolted to his feet. He fought the temptation to pace.

Instead, he gave his mother a tight smile. "Should I get the grill started?"

"Yes, please. Potatoes are baking in the oven." She addressed Mackenzie. "Are you okay with baked potatoes?"

"I love them."

"I do, too. I fried some bacon for breakfast and chopped up the leftovers. We'll have loaded potatoes tonight. Now, what was I saying?"

Cade didn't want to listen to his mother rave about Ty to Mackenzie. Couldn't the woman see those two would be all wrong for each other?

He needed to intervene. "Mackenzie, I have some questions about training Tulip. Would you want to join me while I grill the food?"

"Sure. I can do that." She lifted Tulip off her lap. The dog stretched out each hind leg on the couch, then worked her way over to Christy and settled on her lap to finish her nap.

He led the way to the kitchen, took out the wrapped trays of kabobs from the fridge and carried them to the sliding door to the back deck, where they kept the grill. The house had been built on a hill. A walkout basement below the deck was finished with extra bedrooms for guests. The deck ran the length of the home, and it boasted views of the huge backyard that trailed off into a forest.

Two deer—young does from the looks of it—grazed near the woods.

"This is beautiful." She headed straight to the deck rail and leaned her forearms on it. She smiled as she took in the view. "So peaceful."

"It is." He opened the cover and fired the grill. Then he joined Mackenzie and looked out over the lawn, too.

"What did you want to ask me?"

He'd forgotten about that. "Um, her vest. Should I put it on her when I bring her to the construction site in the morning?"

"Not unless you're actively working with her."

"Okay."

What now?

"Did you grow up here?" she asked.

"I did." He straightened, pointing to the far right corner of the yard. "Ty and I used to have a fort in the woods. It was an old hunting blind my dad set up for us. There's a trail to it over there. We'd stuff our pockets full of granola bars and race each other. The games we would play." He shook his head as the fond memories flooded him. "The fort became a pirate ship, a castle, even a penthouse in the city. We hammered out the rules, fought like feral cats and had a great time."

"Is it still there?"

"No, Dad tore it down after Ty got his driver's license. We'd given up on it years before. Got too cool and too busy for our games."

"A fort sounds like fun. So does having a brother—except for the feral-cat-fighting part."

He chuckled. The sun glinted off her long hair. "No siblings, huh?"

"Nope. Just me."

"You grew up in South Dakota."

"You remembered." She shifted to give him a smile. "Yes, we lived in Rapid City. Dad worked at the company he's about to retire from, and Mom had odd jobs. I didn't have a fort or playhouse, but I got to go to the training center to help him take care of the dogs all the time, and that more than made up for it."

"Is that why you went into veterinary care?"

"It's part of it. I hate seeing anything suffer. Even when I was young, Dad took in rescue animals temporarily to help get them adjusted. I became well acquainted with the typical injuries—physical and emotional—they had."

"Where is your mom now?"

"I have no idea." Her gaze slid away.

Her clipped tone alerted him to change the subject. "When do you think Tulip will be able to visit the nursing home? Nana is really looking forward to meeting her."

Her face cleared. "The earliest? Three weeks. We need to get her used to the wheelchair and have the training session at the nursing home. It wouldn't be fair to Tulip to throw her in a situation without teaching her how to deal with all the sounds, smells and obstacles."

"I see your point."

"She also needs to be able to ignore a pill on the floor when you say 'leave it.' And she needs practice meeting other dogs and other people when out and about. In order to get certified, she needs to be able to do *all* the commands, and she hasn't learned them all."

"Do you think she'll be able to pass the test when the time comes?"

Straightening her arms so the tips of her fingers touched the rail, she nodded. "Yes, I do. But don't rush it. Don't rush her. She's lost her owner, lived with me for a while and now she's settling in to another home. It's a lot to deal with in a short time."

"She's happy here."

"I know. And I want her to stay happy here. We need to think of her needs, too."

Mackenzie was right. He'd been so caught up in wanting to help Nana that he'd overlooked Tulip's needs. The dog did everything they asked of her and more. Sure, she was smart and trainable, but she was also their pet.

Why was he in such a rush, anyhow? Yes, Nana was getting worse, but there wasn't any indication she'd pass away in the immediate future.

God, I can't seem to slow down. I'm never satisfied with what's in front of me. I always have to do more, be better. And for what?

If he didn't get a grip on his restlessness, he might push Tulip too hard. And then Nana wouldn't get to enjoy the dog. The training schedule they were on would have to be good enough. He'd follow Mackenzie's lead. She was the expert, after all.

Chapter Five

～

Mackenzie couldn't believe how much had changed in a few short weeks. Today was the grand opening of Jewel River Veterinary Service, and she'd already given two cats and three dogs routine checkups and shots. She'd also cleaned an infected scrape on a schnauzer. The poor dog had tangled with a wild animal over the weekend. Several locals had stopped in for the free cookies and coffee, and they'd left with coupons for 20 percent off their first visit.

She hoped all of them would use the coupons. While today had been bustling, Wednesday and Friday only had half the appointments filled.

"Mind if I take my lunch?" Greta Dell, the receptionist in her early twenties she'd hired, stood and stretched her back.

"Go ahead." Mackenzie smiled at the pretty woman with springy curls and big brown eyes. Greta had been a good hire. She loved animals and had a sunny nature. All morning, she'd made the pet owners comfortable. Sure, she could be chatty, but Mackenzie figured it was better for business than if she was curt. "I'll stay up front until you're finished."

After today, she'd lock the clinic for the lunch hour, but since this was the open house, Mackenzie was keeping it open for anyone to drop in and check out the facilities. She had too much nervous energy to eat, anyhow.

"Greta, will you tell Emily she can take her lunch, too?" Mackenzie asked. Emily Fulton had two years of experience as a vet tech. She didn't have to be told what to do, and she had a nurturing touch with the animals. Another good hire.

"I'm happy to, Dr. Howard." Greta snatched a tote from under the desk and headed down the hall to where the small break room was located. Mackenzie had insisted on outfitting the room with a sink, microwave, refrigerator, coffeemaker and small table that seated four. Her staff would need the quiet spot to recharge.

She gave Greta's office chair a longing glance. She'd been on her feet since seven this morning, and although it was only one, tiredness seeped into her bones.

The front door opened, and all thoughts of sitting fled. She pasted on her brightest smile as she waited for the newcomers to round the corner into view. To her surprise, Christy, Cade and Tulip, wearing her therapy-dog vest, arrived.

"We just had to stop by and say hi." Christy handed the leash to Cade and hurried around the counter to give Mackenzie a hug. Then she stepped back, keeping her hands at Mackenzie's shoulders, and beamed. "You did it. This place looks amazing, and I've heard you were busy all morning."

She blinked, overwhelmed at the warm welcome and the fact people were actually talking about the clinic. "Yes, we've had a full morning. I have a few more appointments this afternoon, too."

Tulip sat quietly next to Cade, and Mackenzie came out from behind the counter to greet them. She bent to pet the little dog. "Well, hello there, Tulip. Look at you sitting so nicely. I'm honored you came all this way to check out the new clinic. You look spiffy in your vest."

The dog's tail wagged as she remained seated, and Cade took a treat out of his pocket to give to her. She gobbled it up.

Mackenzie laughed, stroking her fur. Then she straightened and found herself looking directly into Cade's shimmering eyes.

"Congratulations," he said with a light drawl. "This place looks great."

"Thank you. It's nice of you to come check it out." Their support meant more to her than either would ever know. They were the only two friends she had in Jewel River at this point.

"We brought a clinic-warming present, too, Mackenzie." Christy's face glowed with excitement.

"You didn't have to do that." What in the world had they brought?

"It's outside. Two planters with flowers. Cade set them on either side of the door, but feel free to move them wherever you want."

"Oh, that's so thoughtful." She hadn't considered adding flowers to the front entrance. Wasn't much into decorating. "Thank you."

"You're welcome."

"I told Mom to check with you first, so don't feel like you have to keep them if they aren't your thing," Cade said. Did she detect a touch of concern in his gaze?

"They *are* my thing. I just never thought to buy them. I appreciate it. Truly."

Christy shot him a smug smile. They'd obviously argued over it. Imagine that. Arguing over giving her a gift. There was a first time for everything.

"Have you gotten any more use out of the trailer?" Cade kept an eye on Tulip as Christy retreated to the counter and selected one of the pamphlets Mackenzie kept for clients.

"Actually, yes. Erica and Dalton Cambridge had me come out last Wednesday. I'll be going to Winston Ranch regularly to check the cattle and vaccinate them." She was thrilled.

Having the largest ranch in several counties on her herd-health plan boosted her confidence.

"Did I hear Winston Ranch?" Christy called over her shoulder. "Did you see their event center? It's ideal for wedding receptions."

"Ignore her." Cade shook his head.

"Your brother set up an appointment for me to come out to his ranch on Thursday."

"I'm not surprised. By the way, I like this look on you." He moved his finger up and down to indicate her outfit—jeans, orthopedic sneakers and a lab coat. She'd braided her hair to keep it out of her way.

Heat shot up her neck. Was he poking fun? As usual, she wore no makeup. The most generous thing she could say about her uniform was that the lab coat gave her an air of authority. She wore it to protect her clothes from all of the animal hair and secretions she dealt with on a daily basis.

"You look like a doctor in it." He grinned.

"Good, because I am a doctor in it." Bantering with him was easy.

The door opened again, and to her surprise, her dad appeared. He approached with his arms wide and lifted her off her feet in a hug.

"You did it, Mackenzie." He set her down and took the place in. "I'm proud of you."

"Thanks, Dad." Her heart filled with pride. She'd been positive he wouldn't be able to make it back to Jewel River until Wednesday—yet, here he was. "Dad, this is Christy and Cade Moulten."

Both mother and son stood behind her. Christy had picked up Tulip.

"Hi, I'm Patrick Howard. We finally meet." He shook Cade's hand first, then turned to Christy. "Nice to meet you, too."

"What a lovely surprise for your daughter." Christy gave Patrick the attentiveness she showed everyone. "Are you in town for good? Cade's been telling me about the training center you're opening."

"I am." Her dad shoved his hands in his pockets as he rocked back on his heels. "I'm itching to get started with the renovations."

"Where will you be staying?" Christy asked.

"I'm renting a small house around the corner."

"The one on Adams Street?"

"That's the one."

Cade hitched his head to the side for Mackenzie to join him. They moved to the corner of the waiting area.

"Do you want me to set up another visit with one of the more rural ranchers?"

Yes, she wanted to meet the other ranchers, but no, she didn't want to have to rely on Cade to do it. And that was stupid. She couldn't let her ego get in the way of her business. Their morning at Triple B Ranch had gone well. Cade had stayed in the background and let her handle Marv. The drive there and back had calmed her nerves, too, as they'd chatted and gotten to know each other.

What could she possibly have against this guy? Nothing. All Cade had done for her since their very first phone call was offer her opportunities.

"I've been to most of the local ranches," she said. "There are still several I'd like to see eventually. But for now, I'm good."

Her cell phone rang, and she answered it without checking the caller.

As soon as she heard "Hello, darling," Mackenzie felt the blood drain from her face. Her knees went wobbly. With a sharp whoosh, she exhaled and willed herself to stand tall. She would not let this call ruin her grand opening.

Her mother had found her.

It wasn't as if she was in hiding, but Mackenzie hadn't expected to hear from her. Especially not today, of all days.

"Why are you calling?" Her voice sounded sharp to her ears. *Calm down. It's just a phone call.*

"To congratulate you on your big day, of course."

She hated the burst of hope spouting at her mother's words. Hated that she still craved her approval. Hated that a part of her still needed her mom's approval.

"How did you find out about it?" The words were clipped. Tone? Ice-cold. She didn't know how else to handle this woman who had caused her so much pain.

"A mother keeps tabs on these things." A nervous undercurrent rode under the role of *proud mom* she was trying to convey. It was on the tip of Mackenzie's tongue to say she only kept tabs when she wanted something.

"I'm kind of busy here." She shifted her weight to one hip.

"I'm sure you are. We can catch up later, Bumblebee."

"Don't call me that." Her lungs seemed to be clenching. If she held the phone any tighter, she'd crush it.

"Fine, *Mackenzie*." Her mother laughed as if it was all a big joke. Maybe it was. Maybe acting like a mother was all one big joke to the woman.

"I've got to go." Mackenzie readied to end the call.

"I'll call you later."

"Don't bother."

"It's important."

Mackenzie clenched her jaw, glanced up at the ceiling and counted to three. "Fine. I'll be done at five thirty."

"I'll call you then."

Mackenzie ended the call, closed her eyes and mentally

prayed. *God, please let her forget to call. Distract her. Anything. I can't go through this again.*

Fascinated, Cade watched as Mackenzie talked on the phone. He'd never seen this side of her—tense, upset. Who was calling to bother her so much? An ex-boyfriend?

When the call ended, Mackenzie seemed to morph back to her normal self. Cade wanted to put his arm around her, to comfort her, but it wouldn't be appropriate. "Are you all right?"

She turned to him, and he'd never seen eyes so full of suppressed hurts. She tried to hide them, but they were there, making him wonder what had caused her so much pain. "I'm fine."

Patrick and Christy stepped forward to join them. Tulip sniffed a mint someone had dropped.

"Leave it," Christy said sharply. Tulip ignored the mint and headed to Mackenzie, then sat at her feet, looking up at her. Mom gave her a treat. Cade was impressed the dog left the mint. The take-it and leave-it commands had been last week's training focus. He and his mom had been working hard with her, and it was clearly paying off.

"Did *you* tell Mom about the grand opening?" Mackenzie opened her hands as she spoke to her father.

"No, I didn't." Patrick shrugged, maintaining eye contact with her. "I thought about telling her, but after our conversation a few weeks ago, I decided not to. Why? Was that her?"

"Yes, it was her. If you didn't tell her, how did she know I moved and that my grand opening is today?" She rubbed her forearms.

Tulip began to whine softly and nuzzled her leg. She bent and picked up the dog, holding her close to her chest. Tulip lifted her little head to try to lick Mackenzie's chin, but she stopped her with a "No lick."

If Cade had any doubts about Tulip bringing comfort to someone in pain, they'd been silenced. The pup had a knack for knowing when someone needed emotional support.

"Maybe your mother saw your website?" Christy's sympathetic tone rang loud and clear. That was one thing about his mom, she was good at making people feel better in rough situations. "I checked it out, and I loved it."

Mackenzie's face cleared, and she nodded. "I'm sure you're right. I wasn't expecting her to call. I wish I'd had a warning."

Patrick had the look of a parent ready to lecture, so Cade tugged on Mackenzie's sleeve. "Let's talk a minute."

Her eyes narrowed with doubts, but she allowed him to lead her out of the waiting area, down the hall to the back room where Tulip's training sessions were held.

Once the door closed behind them, he turned to face her and searched her eyes.

"Is there anything I can do?" he asked. "You're upset."

"I'm not upset." Did she even know she was lying? "I'm... I was surprised. That's all."

"I don't know what you need, but..." He wasn't sure what to say. All he knew was that the unflappable Mackenzie had gotten a shock, and he hated seeing her like this. "I'm here if you need me."

She tilted her head slightly and studied him through questioning eyes.

"Most of my life's together, Cade. I tell myself it's together, but then she barges back into my life and... I feel it threaten to come apart." She shook her head, cuddling Tulip closer. "I appreciate your support. I do. And if there was anything that you could help with, I'd tell you. But this is a heart thing."

A heart thing.

He had one of those, too.

"I pray, but I'm so angry and bitter about my mother, I don't seem to make any progress."

He wanted to find out what her mom did to hurt her, but he couldn't. Asking a question like that would mean opening himself to questions she might ask him. Ones he wouldn't answer.

He doubted he had the capacity to emotionally deal with them beyond what he'd already done.

Her mother had obviously made mistakes. He'd made his share of them, too.

"Don't let it ruin your day. The clinic opening has been a success. Hold on to that."

She glanced at him and stroked Tulip's fur. "Thanks."

"Why don't you go to the break room for a few minutes? Get a cup of coffee or something and relax? Mom and I will man the front desk until you're feeling yourself again."

"That's nice of you, but—"

"Ten minutes, Mackenzie. Take a break."

He pinpointed the exact moment she stopped fighting it.

"Maybe you're right." She set Tulip on the ground and handed Cade the leash. "If someone comes in, though, come and get me."

"I will." Good. She'd agreed to take a few minutes for herself. As she led the way, it hit him how much moving here and opening this practice meant to her. She had high expectations for herself. He did for himself, too. And it seemed both of them had prioritized their careers over their personal lives.

He knew why he had. But why had Mackenzie?

Another question he wasn't willing to ask. They were better off leaving all those questions unanswered and sticking with their priorities—their careers.

At five thirty, Mackenzie opened the door to her house and strode directly to her bedroom to change. All afternoon, she'd put the impending phone call out of her mind to greet visitors and treat her four-legged patients. But when she, Greta and Emily cleaned the clinic after closing at five, her mother's call was all she could think about. She was going to have to make it clear to Bonnie Howard that she wasn't welcome in Jewel River. At least her mom hadn't shown up here with no warning the way she'd done in the past.

Maybe her mom would forget about calling her.

Mackenzie's phone rang.

Of course not.

She popped in her wireless earphones, took a deep breath and answered the call. "Yes?"

"Hello to you, too." Her mother's laugh sounded forced. "It's been a long time since we've caught up."

Not long enough in Mackenzie's opinion.

Straightening, she decided to play along. It wouldn't kill her to be civil. She dropped the combative tone and attempted to loosen her tight muscles by stretching her neck side to side. "Okay, you go first. Where have you been living?"

"Santa Fe."

"What are you doing there?" Mackenzie hoped her mother had a job, but from past experience, she couldn't assume she was currently employed.

"I'm—I was—the creative assistant for a gallery. Hand-made jewelry. Gorgeous pieces."

Was? Just as she'd feared.

"You're not working there anymore?" Mackenzie was too keyed up to sit down. Instead, she hustled to the kitchen and opened the refrigerator. Nothing. She should have stopped by Dixie B's for takeout before coming home. Or casually popped over to the Moultens' place. Christy seemed the type to have supper planned every night. The kebabs Cade had grilled had been delicious.

As if she'd ever just drop in on them. Wasn't going to happen, not with her feelings moving in the direction of liking Cade a little too much. He'd been supportive earlier. Perceptive. He'd known the exact thing to say to make her feel better. The break he'd insisted she take had helped her get back to a better frame of mind.

A girl could rely on a guy like him in a time of crisis.

Her mother coughed. "Um, technically, no."

What did that mean? "And not technically?"

"Well…" The sounds of traffic came through the phone. "The economy took a downturn, and Sherelle had to make some tough choices."

In other words, she'd been fired.

"I'm sorry to hear that." Mackenzie was sorry. Because now it meant Bonnie Howard would become her problem.

"I have options."

Sure, she did. Most likely her mother had one option—coming to Jewel River. Mackenzie was merely her mother's fallback—her last line of hope when life fell apart. Too bad it fell apart so regularly.

"You're not coming here." Mackenzie couldn't deal with the emotional pain it would bring. Not this time. These extended visits always started out okay, but then she'd get lured into believing Mom actually wanted to spend time with her. She'd fool herself into thinking her mother really, truly cared. And she'd end up empty and sad after her mother left—on to a new life, big adventures, exciting people.

"Who said anything about coming there?" Her bright voice told Mackenzie that was exactly what she'd been thinking.

"I know you. You find me when you have nowhere else to go."

"That's not fair, Bumblebee."

"I told you not to call me that." She looked up at the ceiling and ground her teeth together. "Dad doesn't need you mooching off him, either. There aren't any creative jobs in this area. You'd be bored in eleven days. Tops."

"Your father...he's there?"

She brought her palm to her forehead. Why had she let that piece of info slip out?

"Yes, and he's busy. He doesn't need any distractions right now."

"I see." Gone was the sunny, hopeful tone her mom had carefully curated over the years. "I'm not a distraction."

"Yes, you are."

"I wouldn't be mooching—"

"It's all you ever do."

"You think I take advantage of you?" Her pained tone would not make Mackenzie feel guilty.

"Yes. That's exactly what I think." It was a relief to spell it out.

"And here I thought we could have a good catch-up session."

"We are." A good catch-up session? Mackenzie could barely handle talking on the phone with her. To have her show up here would be unbearable. She hated that she had to be so blunt, but she'd been hurt too many times.

"I meant in person," Mom said. "It would be nice to spend some quality time together."

Exactly as she'd feared. Mom did plan on coming there. Her emotions skipped the offended phase and went straight to sad. Her throat felt scratchy as she held back the bad memories.

"It's not quality time when it always ends the same way," Mackenzie said quietly. This conversation would be easier if she could get rid of the hurt little girl inside her and channel the angry adult instead, the way she usually did when dealing with her mother. But anger eluded her.

"What are you talking about?"

"Don't act like you don't know." Mackenzie left the kitchen and stood by the front window to stare at her lawn. "It's all hugs and catching up until you get restless. Then the real reason you're spending time with me reveals itself. Money. It never takes long for you to latch on to a new scheme in a new city, and I'm the one who has to fund it."

"That's not true."

It wasn't true? She let out an incredulous laugh. *That's better.* She was no longer on the verge of tears.

"Buffalo, New York," Mackenzie said. "The radio station assistant position. Two thousand dollars to help with the move and rent. You promised you'd pay me back."

"You said there was no hurry."

Pressure began to build in her temples. "Ashville, North Carolina. You were excited about being a tour guide for the brewery, or was it a winery? I can't remember. Fifteen hundred dollars, again, for the move and rent. You still haven't paid me back."

"If you didn't mean there wasn't a hurry, you shouldn't have said it."

Mackenzie cupped her hands behind her neck and stretched her elbows to the sides. The tightness in her upper back eased slightly. This woman pushed her buttons and didn't even know she was doing it.

"New Orleans. Bakery assistant. You raved about making king cakes and beignets. I gave you three thousand dollars. To get you started. First and last month's rent. That money's long gone."

"New Orleans is an expensive place to live," she said softly.

"What do you really want from me, Mom?" She was tired

of this game. Had promised herself she'd never get suckered into it again. Yet, here they were, having this conversation.

"I miss you. I saw online that the clinic was opening, and I figured I'd tell you how proud I am of you."

The words simultaneously touched her and repelled her. She used to think her mother could do no wrong.

Mackenzie liked to think of herself as a forgiving person, as someone who didn't expect perfection. But her mother had crossed too many lines. All the lines, really.

The woman had let her down every single time she'd shown up unannounced to *catch up* and *spend quality time together*. It always ended the same. With Mackenzie's hard-earned money driving away and a false hope that this time would be different.

It never was.

"Thank you." Mackenzie put no feeling behind the words. She couldn't. Her mom didn't only ask for money and take it and run, she also went silent for months—sometimes years—and barely responded to Mackenzie's calls or texts.

Bonnie Howard's words held no meaning for her anymore.

It was too bad. If they had a normal relationship—a real one—it would have been nice to have a good chat with her mom, to share the ins and outs of the grand opening. Feel the love of a mother. It had been a long, exciting day. But what would be the point? Mom reached out when she needed something, and as soon as she got it, forgot Mackenzie existed. It was just the way life worked with her.

"Give it a week or two," her mother said. "You'll change your mind. I want to see your new place. We can buy rugs or curtains or whatever you need. Spend some time together."

"I don't need rugs or curtains." She did, but the last person she'd go shopping with was her mother. Christy would be a much better choice.

"It wouldn't be for long. A few days. A week, tops."

The nerve of this woman! Hadn't she heard a word Mackenzie said? The fact her mother thought she could stay with her after all the pain she'd put her through was mind boggling.

"I said no."

Neither spoke for a while. This whole routine was too predictable.

"I guess having your mom camp out on your couch is too much for you." The teasing lilt boiled Mackenzie's blood.

"Save your guilt trip. It won't work on me."

"I don't know what I did, but I hope I can make it up to you soon."

She didn't know what she did? And what did she mean by soon? Mackenzie squeezed her eyes shut, trying not to react.

"I'm busy. I have ranches to visit and pets to treat."

"I know you do." Her tone reverted to the optimistic one Mackenzie recognized all too well. Her plans were clearly in motion, leaving Mackenzie no choice in the matter. "We'll find time to hang out. I can work around your schedule."

She was too tired to argue. She'd said all she'd planned on saying. There was no way she'd play along with her mother's weird games. If the woman thought Mackenzie was okay with her staying with her and would fit her into her schedule, she was dead wrong.

She'd been through this one too many times. She'd given all she could give. This time her mother was on her own.

Chapter Six

"I'm impressed with how quickly Tulip mastered the release and place commands. It's obvious you've been working with her." Mackenzie was crouching to pet Tulip in the back room of the clinic the following Monday evening. Cade hadn't seen her since the previous week's training session, and he wanted to ask about her mother and if she'd been out to any more ranches. But not with his mom next to him.

He also wanted to draw her into his arms. Ask her how her day was and listen to everything on her mind. To say she'd been dominating his thoughts was an understatement.

Instead, he glanced at his mother. She gave him a proud smile.

"We're motivated," Mom said. "Trudy's memory is slipping a little more each day. We really want her to be able to enjoy Tulip before things get too bad."

It was the first time his mother had mentioned any concerns about how quickly Nana's mental state was declining. She should know. She visited her almost every day. Cade hadn't wanted to face the fact Nana had been having more bad days than good lately. Last Wednesday, when he'd stopped by, she'd been fine. But Friday's visit with Ty had been a bust—she'd barely been able to keep her eyes open.

A heavy sadness weighed on his chest. What if they

trained Tulip, and it ended up being for nothing? He'd seen the late-stage dementia patients in the nursing home enough to know that many of them had almost no awareness of what went on around them.

He and Mom should have trained a dog months ago. Before Nana's Alzheimer's had worsened. Seeing his vibrant grandmother diminished and confused always punched him in the gut. He missed the caring woman he'd taken for granted for far too long.

"I understand," Mackenzie said, rising. "Tulip's training is coming along fine. No need to worry. She'll be ready soon. I asked Dad to observe our session tonight. He should be here in a few minutes."

"Rumor around town is that your clinic is a smashing success," Mom said. "Everyone's relieved to have you taking care of their pets."

"Thank you. It's been chaotic getting everything ready. I, for one, am glad the appointments filled up so quickly after the grand opening. The flowers at the entrance really make it welcoming, too. Thank you again for bringing them over."

"You've already thanked me ten times," Mom said cheerily. "We couldn't be happier to have you here, Mackenzie."

Cade almost raised his eyebrows at her use of the word *we*, but he didn't. He *was* happy to have her here. Even if it made him uncomfortable at times.

Mackenzie was transparent. What you saw was what you got. Cade, on the other hand, hid himself behind a socially acceptable exterior. And lately, he'd been tempted to let down his guard. Allow Mackenzie to catch a glimpse of the real him, the one he'd been trying to hide since New York. He had a feeling she'd already glimpsed it, but if she hadn't? She'd hate that side of him as much as he did. He'd just have to keep it under wraps.

"Let's see how she adapts to the wheelchair." Mackenzie pointed her thumb over her shoulder in the direction of the door. "I'll bring it in. If she barks at it, use the quiet command. A lot of dogs feel threatened by strange objects. We have several strategies to help them overcome their fears."

Mackenzie hustled away, and Cade turned to his mom. "Is Nana getting worse?"

Her expression fell. "Yes. It might be temporary. Her immune system could be fighting something or maybe she's tired, but she's been out of it lately. Has she been okay when you've dropped by?"

"For the most part. I haven't been getting over there as often as I should. I'll drop by to see her tomorrow."

"Here we are." Mackenzie pushed a wheelchair through the door. Tulip immediately began barking at it.

"Quiet," Mom said to the dog. She stopped barking, but then she started again.

"She feels insecure around it. That's normal," Mackenzie said. "I'll move it out of sight, and when she's calm, let's try the place command."

"In the bed over there?" Mom pointed to the dog bed placed off to the side.

"Yes, it was her bed when she lived with me, so she's familiar with it."

Cade watched as his mother nodded and gave her the command. Tulip followed Christy to the small bed and got into it. His mother praised her and gave her a treat.

"Good job." Mackenzie watched the process from where she stood in front of the wheelchair. "Now have her lie down."

"Lie down." Mom used the hand signal. Tulip obeyed and got another treat.

"Nice work, Christy." Mackenzie watched to make sure Tulip stayed put. "I'm going to have you stand a few feet away from her. I'll slowly move the chair your way. Considering the fact she initially barked at it, I'm expecting her to get antsy, maybe even circle around as I bring the chair close to her. If that happens, your job is to remind her to lie down. Are you ready?"

His mom nodded. Cade's gut tightened. What if Tulip didn't get used to the wheelchair? Nana would never get a chance to enjoy the dog. This low-grade tension constantly made him feel like time was running out.

Mackenzie slowly pushed the wheelchair to the side of the room. Then she brought it over near Christy, and Tulip began to shake. As she wheeled it near Tulip, the dog got up to pace around the bed and never took her eyes off the wheelchair.

"Lie down." Mom's voice wavered.

"Speak normally, Christy. Stay relaxed. She gets her cues from you." Mackenzie then turned the wheelchair and walked it past Cade around the room and right back to the bed. Tulip began to shake, but this time, she didn't get up, nor did she bark.

Patrick arrived and stood by the door watching them. Cade nodded to him in greeting.

Mackenzie took a few more laps, brought the wheelchair to the edge of the bed, wheeled it back and handed it to Cade. "I'm going to have you push it around for a few minutes."

It was on the tip of his tongue to ask why, but he simply took the handles. "Where to?"

"Anywhere you'd like, but make sure you get it close to Tulip. We want her to accept it as a normal, non-threatening object in her life." Mackenzie must have noticed her father. She waved to him. "We're getting her used to the wheelchair."

"I see." Patrick's eyes crinkled in good humor.

Cade didn't know how he felt about being watched by her father, but he began to push the wheelchair anyway. He stopped it close to the bed and moved it around the room. Mackenzie held her phone to video Tulip.

"Keep going, Cade," Patrick said. "Make a smaller circle with it, get it close to her several times."

He felt kind of foolish, but he continued to move the wheelchair back and forth and up to Tulip.

"There. You see?" Mackenzie pressed the button on the phone and pointed to the dog. "She's decided—for the moment anyway—that it's nothing to get worked up about. See how she's ignoring it? Keep going, Cade."

He kept pushing the chair, but he could tell Mackenzie was right. Tulip rested her chin on her front paws as she lay in the bed. She kept an eye on the chair, but she was no longer shaking.

"Okay, that's enough. You can stop pushing the wheelchair. Christy, you can free Tulip from the place command." Mackenzie slipped her phone into her back pocket as Mom told Tulip to release, then lavished the dog with praise and treats. Mackenzie grinned. "Ten minutes. That's all it took."

Patrick moved farther into the room. "Let's see how she does with a stranger approaching. Christy, have her walk to the center of the room with you. Then tell her to sit."

His mom obeyed, and Tulip obliged.

"I'm going to come over and shake your hand. If she moves out of her sit command, remind her to sit and give her the physical cue, okay?"

"Sure thing." His mom's cheeks were rosy, but she commanded Tulip to the center of the room and had her sit. Thankfully, the dog walked loosely on the leash next to her, the way they'd been insisting on their evening walks.

Patrick approached Christy and extended his hand. "How are you doing today?"

Mom shook it, and they chatted for a few seconds while Tulip sat calmly beside her.

"Nice," Patrick said. He crouched to pet the dog. "Hi there, Tulip." Then he straightened. "She's doing well. Next week, she might revert to barking at the wheelchair, but this was good progress."

Cade didn't want to wait another week for her to encounter the wheelchair. "What if we took the wheelchair home with us? Worked with her on it for a while each day?"

Mackenzie tilted her chin as if trying on the idea and slowly nodded. She glanced at her dad, who waited for her decision.

"I don't see a problem with it," she said. "What do you think, Dad?"

"I'm all for it."

"Ten minutes at a time. That should be enough." A frown line grew above her nose. "If she gets to a point where she's not responding to it at all, would you want to teach her to walk beside the wheelchair, too?"

"Yes," Cade and Christy said in unison.

Mackenzie met her father's gaze, and they both chuckled.

"Good," Mackenzie said. "Here, let us show you what to do."

With a leash in her hand, Mackenzie sat in the wheelchair and explained how to hold it for the dog to be far enough away from the chair. "You want her to go at your pace, and you want her to learn how to avoid the wheels. Being walked by someone in a wheelchair isn't something I anticipate her needing to do, but it will help protect her when she's at the nursing home."

"Anything that will keep our princess safe," Christy said. "Right, Cade?"

He nodded. For once, he agreed with his mother.

"Yes," he said. "Mackenzie, how much longer will we have to wait?"

"For what?"

"For her to get certified?" He'd been trying not to push the dog. Trying to think of her as just their pet. But she *was* training to be a therapy dog, and he longed for his grandmother to enjoy her. "I want Nana to meet her."

"Dad, I'll let you take this one."

"She's almost there," Patrick said. "Work with her this week. Be relaxed, praise her and give her treats when she succeeds. Get her out around other people. Make her sit at your feet while you talk to them and do the same if they have a dog."

"Do you think she'll be ready for a test run at the nursing home next week?" Mackenzie asked.

"I do."

"I'll call them and see if we can bring her there for training. Are you both available on Tuesday afternoon?"

He and his mom nodded.

Cade's spirits lifted. Finally.

"Good," Mackenzie said. "That's settled."

She began chatting with his mom, and Patrick approached him. "I looked into the building you mentioned to Mackenzie."

Cade racked his brain, and then he remembered. "Oh, right. For the people to stay at when they get their dogs."

"Yes." He nodded. "It's a little too off the beaten path. You wouldn't happen to know any real estate agents who could help me out, would you?"

Cade rattled off the names he trusted. "The property across the street from here might be an option."

"What do you mean?"

"You could build something to accommodate them."

"Wouldn't it be expensive?"

"Probably. But it's worth looking into."

"I appreciate it." Patrick clapped him on the shoulder. "You've helped both me and Mackenzie more than you know."

Guilt crept over him. *You think I'm a good person, but I'm not.*

He didn't deserve Patrick's thanks. Or his daughter. And he'd better not forget it.

"Who is this?" As soon as Mackenzie entered her dad's building the next day at noon, she spotted the German shepherd. The past couple of weeks had been a rollercoaster—tough, exciting, fantastic and predictable—all at the same time. The full days at the clinic had her missing coming home to Tulip. She'd been seriously considering getting a dog of her own, but she wasn't home much. She had no time for pets. No time for a boyfriend. Not even for a guy like Cade.

Why her spirits plunged at the thought, she didn't want to evaluate. Everything was going well. She should be happy.

Dad grinned. "Meet Charger."

"Where did you get him? And when?" She approached the dog and let him sniff her closed hand before petting him. His tail wagged as his big eyes looked up at her with affection. "He's a sweetie. And from the looks of it, already on his way to being well-behaved."

"Leslie called this morning, and when she explained his situation, I drove out there straight away. He's full of energy, but a smart dog like him needs a job to do. He'll be easy to train, despite his bad habits." Dad had a soft spot for energetic large dogs who proved too much for their owners. Like her, though, he'd opted not to own one since he wasn't home much. But now he would be. Dad ruffled the dog's head. "He turns one in October."

"A puppy."

"Moldable. I'm hoping he'll be able to help settle the dogs we train here. They do better when they have a good role model around."

"Where has Charger been living?" Mackenzie continued to pet him. He ate up the attention.

"A young couple bought him as a puppy, but they brought home a newborn last week and can't meet his needs."

"That's sad." She rubbed behind his ears.

"It's better that they realize it now." Dad tilted his head and watched her. "You're doing a good job training Tulip. You settling in at the clinic okay?"

"Thanks. She's been easy to train. And yes, the clinic is booked out for the next couple of weeks. It's amazing how much business even a small town has when it comes to pets."

"I'm sure people in the surrounding towns are making appointments, too."

"True. Now, I just need the mobile vet services to take off. The ranchers I've met around Jewel River seem to be on board with my animal husbandry plan for their cattle. Hopefully, the ranchers in the surrounding area will reach out, too."

"They will." He pointed to the door. "Have you eaten lunch?"

"No. I came straight over when I saw your truck."

"Let's get burgers at Dixie B's."

"Yes."

Ten minutes later, after dropping off Charger and crating him at her father's house, Mackenzie and her dad sat opposite each other in a booth at Dixie B's. The forest green walls held framed pictures of wildlife. The place was hopping for a Tuesday. They both ordered burgers, fries and sodas, then settled in to catch up.

"Have you hired a contractor?" she asked, smiling at the waitress when their drinks arrived.

"Ed McCaffrey is number one on my list if he can fit me in."

"Yeah, I liked him, too. I wish he'd had time for the clinic. The contractor I hired did a good job, but the finish work wasn't the greatest. I touched up some of it myself."

"If you need me to help with anything, say the word."

"I will."

"Have you heard from your mother again?"

"I talked to her the night of the grand opening. Since then? No." She left it at that. "When do you plan on opening the training center?"

"It depends on how quickly the renovations can be finished. Plus, I need a place for the clients to stay. Last night, Cade mentioned the possibility of having something built."

"That might work." A prick jabbed her conscience. Cade had helped her time and again since she moved to town. All he'd ever asked of her was to come out and see his stables. And she hadn't made the time.

She liked being with Cade. He made it all feel easy, and she wasn't an easy person. "By the way, we're set for the training session at the nursing home next Tuesday. Want to join us?"

"Of course I do. Tulip's almost ready. I have a good feeling about that little dog." He grinned. "Have you made any friends yet?"

Cade. Christy. "Some."

"And your free time? Are you relaxing?"

"Yep." It was mostly true. After supper each night, she'd been reading up on the latest recommendations for equine care in case she was thrown into a situation she hadn't handled before.

She still hadn't gotten any emergency calls. Her nerves kept climbing with worry that she'd encounter a problem she couldn't handle. What if she lost a cow or horse due to inexperience? What if it soured the community against her?

The thought had kept her up a night or two.

"Are you *really* taking time for yourself?" His gaze probed her.

They'd had this conversation off and on throughout the years. He worried she was all work and no play.

So what if she was? She liked work. Didn't have much desire to play.

"I watched a show on television last night."

His deadpan stare made her squirm. "Let me guess. A reality show about a veterinarian."

"It's still a show. It counts." Heat rose to her cheeks.

Sighing, he gave his head a slight shake. "There's more to life. Watch one of those romantic movies or get coffee with a friend. Make a life—a real life—here, Mackenzie."

She wanted to tell him she had a real life, but it wasn't true. While she got along well with her employees, she couldn't share with Greta and Emily everything going on in her life, nor did she want to. They were gossip machines.

"Have you been to church?" he asked. Their food arrived. It looked and smelled delicious.

"Not yet. I was waiting for you to get here."

"Okay, then, Sunday we'll go together. I'm sure there are plenty of nice people your age here. Get to know them."

What he was really telling her was to get a life. For the first time in years, she could admit to herself that he was right. The thought of having to put herself out there made her squirm, though. Dad made it all sound easy. But for a girl like her? There was nothing easy about it.

Maybe the first step could be taking Cade up on his offer to tour his stables.

The next time he asked her to stop by, she would.

But what if he didn't?

Then she'd stop by on her own. There was more to life than work. At least, that was what she'd been told.

She liked Cade. But what if getting close to him was a mistake?

The following afternoon, Cade finished his to-do list at the makeshift office on the construction site of the stables and climbed into his truck. He'd reached out to Forestline Adventures again and left a message with their receptionist. He'd called five other companies on his list, too, but none of them were as large or had as many horses as Forestline. With the Fourth of July the day after tomorrow, Cade didn't expect to hear back from any of them until next week at the earliest.

He could have waited to call them, but sometimes people surprised him and were more available during holiday weeks. This didn't happen to be one of those times.

After starting the truck, he cranked the air conditioning. Everything that needed to be done to open Moulten Stables was falling into place. Next on his hot list was to start looking for a manager to hire. Someone with an impeccable record, superior experience in taking care of horses and the credentials to back it all up.

And integrity. The person he hired had to have integrity.

Yeah, like you?

He was trying. Every day for six years, he'd been trying to have integrity.

No matter how hard you try, you'll never have it. You're fooling everyone, but you can't fool yourself.

Grinding his teeth together, he shook away the thoughts. The manager he hired would also have to be okay with living in a small town. Cade drove away and cast a glance toward the huge old house across the road. He'd purchased it last year. It had been sitting empty for months. Everything in it was outdated, but it had good bones. He figured its proximity to the stables made it valuable. Maybe he could throw in free rent to a manager to sweeten the deal.

Ty might be able to suggest someone. Despite being reclusive, his brother had a knack for knowing these things.

The short drive to the nursing home went by in a flash. Part of him dreaded going there. He wished Nana was back at her home, baking cookies and giving him a big old hug. They used to sit at her kitchen table, and she'd ask him and Ty about life and school. He'd tell her everything was fine. But after three or four cookies, he'd open up and confess what was really on his mind.

Right now, what was on his mind was Mackenzie. He tried to push her out of his thoughts, but there she was.

Lately he'd been feeling off. Not queasy or ill—just not himself. Instead of constantly thinking about opening Moulten Stables or studying the stocks he'd invested in or coming up with a new improvement for the ranch, his mind had been glued to one thing—Mackenzie.

She didn't mince words. He got the impression she wasn't one to reveal much, although she'd revealed quite a bit to him over the past month. Her patience awed him. Her attention to detail did, too. As did her unpretentious manner.

He wanted to spend more time with her.

If only he could get Nana's advice. He could use it—and a cookie or two—at the moment. He wasn't fool enough to think that in her current state she'd be able to smooth out his troubles the way she used to, but he still liked being with her. Missed her unconditional love.

A parking spot at the far end of the lot caught his eye, and he backed the truck into it.

Out in the fresh air, he pocketed his keys and pulled back his shoulders. Enough thinking about Mackenzie.

Which Nana was he going to get today? The one who remembered him and was happy to see him? The one with blank eyes and no energy? Or the one lost in the past who didn't recognize him?

Did it matter? He'd handle whatever version was presented, even though the latter two broke his heart.

"Hey there, Cade," Charlene said as he approached her desk. "Miss Trudy is in her room."

"How is she today?"

Charlene winced. "She's tired. But she'll be happy to see you. You always brighten her day."

His spirits sank knowing it was going to be one of those visits where she didn't speak much, and he simply held her hand. He liked when she had color in her cheeks and was sitting in her wheelchair. On good days, she'd know who he was. He'd tell her what was going on around town, and the updates made her smile.

If Charlene's expression told him anything, today would not be that day.

"Thanks for the head's up." He strode down the hall. Besides the disinfectant smell and moans coming from one of the rooms, the place was decent enough.

Her door was open. He still knocked on it before entering. "Hi, Nana."

As he'd feared, she was not in her wheelchair but sitting in the raised hospital bed. She stared out the window with a blank expression, but she turned her head. Her eyes opened wider. "Pete?"

Cade's heart pinched. This wasn't the first time she'd mistaken him for his father. It always hurt, mainly because he wished it was true—that his father was still alive. He'd do about anything to see his dad again. "No, Nana, it's me, Cade."

Her eyelashes fluttered, and her cloudy blue eyes floundered trying to place him.

"Pete's son." He approached her and covered her hand with his.

"Oh, yes." She nodded, but he could tell she was simply going along with him and didn't know who he was. He pulled the chair over to the bed, sat down and took her hand in his again.

"How are you doing today?" he asked.

"I'm pretty good." She gave him a smile. "Did you know Aunt Jo came over yesterday?"

"Aunt Jo? Really?" He raised his eyebrows and kept his tone even. Nana had claimed many times that Aunt Jo had visited her, but Aunt Jo had passed away thirty years ago.

Cade and his mom had learned from the doctors and staff that it was best to stay calm and go along with any delusions. Dementia and Alzheimer's patients couldn't help the changes in their brain and just wanted to feel understood. It would do no good to argue with her.

"Yes, she brought the necklace she promised me." She fingered the neckline of her shirt. The necklace with the cross pendant was there. Nana had worn it every day Cade could remember.

"It's pretty, Nana. Aunt Jo must really love you."

"Oh, she does." She stared at him then, her eyes shining. "She's worried about you, Pete."

His chest grew tight. He always felt uncomfortable when she was like this.

"Next time you see her, tell her there's nothing to worry about." He tried to change the subject. "What did you have for lunch?"

Nana tightened her grip on his hand and implored him with her eyes. "I'm worried, too. Christy's good for you. You should ask that girl to marry you. She can't help it her mama didn't know how to be a parent. Be patient with her, and she'll learn to trust you."

This was new. When Nana's mind retreated to the past, she never mentioned his mother, and Christy and Trudy had been close. Close enough that Cade knew his mom considered Trudy Moulten more of a mother than her own estranged parent.

"I will."

"Good." Nana relaxed back into the pillow with a sigh of contentment and let go of his hand. "Is Dolly okay?"

"Yeah, Dolly's great." Who was Dolly again?

"That dog misses me. Tell your daddy to give her extra attention until I can come home. The doctors should be letting me out any day now. You cuddle Dolly, too, okay?"

"I will." Cade wasn't going to be able to take much more of this. He was already getting choked up, and he'd only been here for a few minutes. "You'll get to see another dog soon. Tulip. She's a Pomeranian. You'll like her. She's tiny, like a little peach puffball."

"Tulip?" She frowned. "I don't remember a dog with that name."

"She's new. You haven't seen her yet."

Her face cleared. "Oh, good. I thought I'd forgotten. I've always liked small dogs."

"She's growing on me." In fact, Cade wished the little

dog was here with them now. She'd sit on his lap and lick his hand and make him feel like he could handle his grandmother thinking he was his father and sharing things from the past he didn't know what to do with.

"Little dogs need to sit on your lap, you know," Nana said. "Don't push her away. You're used to big dogs, but the small ones need your affection."

"I know. I'm learning."

"Good." She closed her eyes, and he took that as his sign to leave.

Then he bent over and kissed her forehead. "Goodbye, Nana. I'll see you in a few days."

"Goodbye, Pete. Don't forget what I said. Christy's good for you."

"Okay."

He left the room. All the way down the hall, he fought a sense of disorientation. It was true that he and Ty resembled their father. He'd have to ask Ty if Nana ever confused him with their dad, too.

"How was she?" Charlene bustled toward him.

"About as good as could be expected."

"I'm sorry, hon." She looked two seconds away from giving him a hug. He couldn't handle one at the moment. Might break the dam of tears he was holding back. "Your mom's been showing us pictures of Tulip, and Mackenzie called to bring her out next Tuesday afternoon. We can't wait to see her. It's so nice of you to offer to bring the little pup when you come visit."

"Anything for Nana." He didn't feel nice. He felt sad. Sad that Nana was here thinking about Dolly, a dog long dead, and giving him dating advice about his own mother.

"We have several seniors who could really use a pick-me-up, too. I think getting to interact with Tulip would make their days brighter."

He hadn't thought about bringing Tulip around to other people in the nursing home. "Yeah, that's what Mom said, too."

"When the time comes, I'll take you to the patients who could use a little pick-me-up." Charlene's expression changed from hopeful to understanding. "Showing the dog to the other seniors might bring you some peace, too, hon." She rubbed his upper arm in compassion.

"I'll think about it." He gave her a tight smile. How would bringing the dog to other elderly people bring *him* peace? All it would do was remind him they'd once been strong, and now they were stuck in a nursing home. At the moment, this entire place depressed him. "Thanks, Charlene. I'm going to take off."

He strode down the hall, through the door and out into the sunshine. The sadness slowly lessened, only to be replaced with questions. Questions he'd never really considered.

He'd always assumed his mom and dad had fallen madly in love, gotten married and lived happily ever after. Sure, he knew the stories they'd told him about Christy arriving in town when she was in high school. About Pete stopping in at the discount clothing store where she worked even though he didn't need any clothes. They'd been opposites—Dad was calm and reserved; Mom was bubbly and outgoing.

But Cade had never considered there'd been any hiccups along the way to their engagement and marriage. Had never really thought of his parents as real people at all. They'd just been Pete and Christy. At one point, though, they'd been individuals with their own problems, their own dreams.

He climbed into the truck and started it. His phone rang.

"Hello?"

"Are you free tomorrow morning?" The voice was female. He didn't recognize it.

"Who's calling?"

"Paris Grove. I'm passing through Jewel River tomorrow, and my father wants me to stop by your new stables."

Paris Grove. Michael Grove's daughter. The CEO of Forestline Adventures was sending his daughter to check out the operation? Why wouldn't he come himself?

"I'll be at the stables in the morning," he said. He wasn't missing this opportunity. "Do you need the address? The property is close to town, but the town itself is off the beaten path."

"Text it to me. I'll find it. I hope it's as good as you told my dad. I plan on taking pictures during the tour."

"Take all the pictures you want." The stables were coming along as scheduled, but he wished she would have called a few weeks from now. Actually, he wished her father would have called. Giving Paris the tour wouldn't be the same as convincing Michael to board their horses with him.

Regardless, this meeting needed to go well. He'd make sure the construction zone was as clean as possible. Highlight all the features that would be added by summer's end. If this was his shot at landing their business, he'd make the most of it.

And if it took his mind off of everything else, all the better. He'd been thinking about Mackenzie too much, worrying about Nana too much. He needed to get his head back where it belonged—on his business.

Chapter Seven

Cade couldn't help wishing he'd be giving Mackenzie the tour of the property this morning instead of Paris. The horse barn, though not finished, was coming along nicely. He'd worked with a designer to select materials to give the finished space a rustic, timeless—and expensive—feel. At the moment, the stalls were roughed in, and the windows and exterior doors had been installed. If Paris would have waited two more weeks to visit, she could have seen the lantern-inspired sconces with textured glass above the door of each stall, along with the special floors he'd picked out, the hooks, the benches—all of it.

In its current shape, the place was unlikely to impress her.

Last night, he'd researched Paris's role with the company. She was the marketing manager, described herself as an aesthetics specialist—whatever that meant—and brand guru. He was under the impression if she didn't think his facility worthy of being photographed, she'd tell her father to use a different boarder.

Cade wanted their business.

He slowly took in the construction site, looking for anything that needed to be cleaned or put away before Paris arrived. The sweet scent of wood shavings filled the air. Nail guns *pop, popped* at the other end of the long barn. A sports drink lay on its side next to an overturned bucket to his left. He picked up both and took them to the crew's trailer.

Once that was finished, he mentally reviewed all of the selling points he'd finalized yesterday. Then he checked his phone—she'd be arriving any minute—took a deep breath and prayed.

Lord, I need this meeting to go well. I've done everything possible to make this property the best it can be. I've spared no expense. Please, let her see what it could be, not what it is.

He strode around the barn, then stopped to look over the grounds. Fencing was being installed at the back of the property to create pastures for the horses. The outdoor arena had been cleared, but it would be a few more weeks before the materials for it would be delivered.

Would Forestline be able to make a decision based on the current shape of the property?

The sound of tires on gravel made him turn. Paris must have arrived. He went back through the barn's large sliding wooden doors, then across the barn aisle and out the opposite set of sliding wooden doors. A large, black SUV came to a stop in front of him.

Showtime. Cade plastered on a confident smile and waited. The passenger door opened, and out stepped a woman in her late twenties who could have graced the cover of any magazine. Thick, wavy black hair bounced past her shoulders and stopped midway down her back. Oversized sunglasses hid her eyes, and dark red lipstick punctuated her heart-shaped lips. Her fitted sheath dress hugged her curves. Dangerously high heels made Cade blink.

The woman knew she'd be touring a construction zone, right?

She whipped out her phone and began snapping pictures. Before he could greet her, she began filming and talking into the phone. "I'm getting the when-you-want-to-escape-it-all vibe. Blue skies. Trees along the back of the property. Pasture for miles. Nothing—and I mean nothing—to do except ignore it all..."

Cade wasn't sure what to do in this situation. Did he interrupt her and introduce himself? Wait for her to finish whatever she was filming? This wasn't one of those live videos on social media, was it?

The choice was made for him when she touched her screen to end the video, slipped it into her small designer purse, shifted her sunglasses to rest on the top of her head and strolled toward him with a wide smile.

"Hello." Her big brown eyes sparkled as she extended her hand. "Paris Grove. You must be Cade Moulten."

In that instant, his nerves disappeared. He knew exactly what to do, what to say and how to handle this woman. Hers was a world he'd mastered during his time in New York.

"Miss Grove. It's a pleasure." Giving her a playful smile, he shook her hand. "I hope your drive was uneventful. Are you hungry? Thirsty?"

"Paris, please," she said. "Yes, uneventful is exactly how I'd describe it. You're on the edge of civilization out here, aren't you? As for your other question, no, thank you. Gerald and I already ate." She looked back over her shoulder and waved to the driver. "Gerald takes me everywhere. He's used to my detours and shenanigans. Best driver in the world."

"Gerald is welcome to join us, or he can stretch his legs around the property."

"He needs a break from me, but that's sweet of you." She shifted her weight and studied him. "You're not what I was expecting."

"Oh, yeah?" He had a good idea what she'd expected. Either a wealthy businessman or a no-nonsense cowboy. He was neither and he was both.

"Yeah, I figured with your Wall Street background, you were playing out a childhood Western fantasy here."

"Sorry, no childhood fantasies involved. I grew up in Jewel River."

"I see." Her eyes twinkled. "Was the city too big for you?"

"Nah," he said with a grin. "My dad died. I came home to take over the ranch."

"My research didn't turn up any of that." She hooked her arm in his, and together they faced the stables. "Hope you don't mind. I need a steady arm to lean on in these heels."

"You don't strike me as the type to need any help at all. You know what you're doing."

"Flatterer." She laughed. "But you can't blame a girl for wanting an excuse to lean on a strong cowboy."

He chuckled, but it was all for show. He had nothing to worry about from Paris Grove. Yes, she was a flirt, but there would never be anything between them. She wasn't his type. Even if she was, his life was here, and she'd be off on a new adventure within twenty-four hours.

Lately, all he could think about was strawberry blond hair and hooded blue eyes.

Over the next hour, he showed Paris the unfinished barn and gave her an overview of the pastures and grounds. As they strolled back to his makeshift office, he described the services the boarding facility would offer. Inside, he pulled out a comfortable chair for her to sit on. He'd brought four of them in last night, in case more people—namely, her father—showed up with her. They both sat, and he directed her attention to the table where his laptop was set up.

Paris pushed her chair back and to the side, then crossed one leg over the other. He angled his chair to face her better.

Then he went through the digital renderings of the finished stables, pastures, riding paths and outdoor arena.

"Who's going to run this place?" she asked. "You?"

"No. I'll be hiring a manager."

"Anyone in mind?"

"I just started the process. I'm looking for an expert with horses. I have high standards."

"That will make our customers happy."

"I know."

"Who else will have access to the stables?"

"We'll have other people boarding their horses here."

"That could be a liability."

He narrowed his eyes slightly, then forced himself to appear open and relaxed. "How so?"

"We provide highly trained, expensive horses to our clients. I'm not sure we want anyone off the street around our investments during the off-season."

He hadn't considered that aspect. The building was one long barn at the moment.

"Your horses will be treated like the prizes they are. No one but my staff will be allowed to take care of them, feed them, ride them or even approach them. Their safety, health and well-being are my primary concern."

"We'll keep that in mind." She opened the folder he'd given her with all the information about Moulten Stables. "When did you say this place would be ready?"

"By September. You can board all of your horses here this winter. Say the word."

"We'll think about it." A knowing smile lifted her lips, then she took out her phone again. "Mind if we get a picture together?"

He hated having his picture taken. Refused to sign up for

any social media accounts. But this was business, and it was obvious social media was Paris's wheelhouse.

"Sure."

They smooshed together, and she raised the phone and clicked a few selfies. Then he walked her back to the SUV, where Gerald was waiting, shook her hand and said goodbye.

They drove away. Paris was probably any other guy's dream girl, but he still would have rather spent the morning with Mackenzie.

His old world—although he'd moved easily within it—had never fulfilled him. And the people he used to spend time with thrived on a busier, louder, more competitive life than he had the stomach for.

So why was he still chasing it?

I'm not. I just want to provide a service to my community, and I need the big clients to fund it.

Did he though? He had a high net worth. *Yes, I need them.* Why was he second-guessing himself?

He wanted to find Mackenzie and tell her how the meeting had gone. Tulip's next training session was too far off to wait. He could drive over to the clinic. But she was busy.

Maybe he should ask Ty his take on the issue of the stables being one building. He could pick his brain about hiring a manager, too.

What time was it? Lunch time at the clinic. A quick call wouldn't hurt.

He pressed Mackenzie's number.

"Hey, Cade. What's up?"

"Just checking in." He wanted to thump his forehead at how lame that sounded.

"How's Tulip doing with the wheelchair? Or have you had a chance to work with her?"

"Mom and I tag-teamed with it last night. Tulip trembled at first but eventually settled down."

"I'm glad."

A long pause ensued.

"Charlene Parker mentioned you set up the training session at the nursing home." Why was he talking about this when he really wanted to tell her about the stables and the meeting?

"Yes, the staff is very accommodating. They seem excited at the prospect of having a therapy dog come around."

"Yeah." He didn't know what he was hoping to accomplish. All he knew was he liked hearing her voice. "Are you going to the Fourth of July festival tomorrow?"

He always enjoyed walking around the booths and food trucks. American flags lined the sidewalks up and down Center Street. The street would be blocked off, with a stage set up at one end for various entertainment throughout the day. Fireworks were scheduled at night, too.

"I don't know. I probably should go. The clinic will be closed, and I don't plan on visiting any ranches unless they have an emergency."

"Why don't you come over to the stables in the morning?"

"You don't give up, do you?" Her teasing tone made his heart skip a beat.

"I don't."

"Okay. You wore me down. What time should I come by?"

"How about nine? I'll stop by Annie's Bakery and get us doughnuts and coffee first."

"Deal. But only if you pick me up a couple of her crullers."

"They're delicious."

"Don't I know it."

"And after, we can go to the festival together."

"Like a date?" she sounded skeptical.

"Sure. Like a date." His heart started pounding. Now he'd gone and done it. He'd crossed his own invisible line—and asked her on a date. It wasn't panic making his pulse race, though. It was excitement.

"I've got a pregnant mare acting funny."

The words stopped Mackenzie cold that evening. Marc Young was on the line. The day had been long. Rather than being tired, though, she'd been keyed up at the prospect of hanging out with Cade tomorrow morning at his stables and going to the festival with him after.

A date. Only a slightly less terrifying thought than this phone call.

"When is your mare due?" She focused on the problem at hand. A pregnant mare acting funny wasn't just a problem—it was her biggest fear.

"In about six weeks." Horses had long gestational periods—ten to eleven months. Since foals gained almost all of their weight toward the end of the pregnancy, Mackenzie hoped the mare wasn't going into premature labor.

"Describe how she's acting." She listened as Marc described Miss Lightning's symptoms. "I'll bring my trailer out right away. What's your address?"

After they ended the call, she typed the address into her phone and grabbed her keys. The drive to the clinic took all of two minutes, and once she'd connected the trailer, she headed out of town to his ranch.

Memories of losing the horse and foal all those years ago crowded her mind. What if this was a similar situation? What if she had to perform surgery and she lost the mother and foal again? It was no secret Marc's mom ran the bakery in town, and his wife owned the gourmet chocolate shop. Mackenzie couldn't afford to mess this up. Couldn't get a bad reputation this early in the game. More than anything, though, she needed to get it right for the horse's sake.

God, I'm scared. It's not like I haven't worked with horses. Dr. Johan insisted I take the lead on several calls. But what if something goes wrong? What if I make the wrong choice? Please, help me!

She wished Tulip was here. Wished she could pet the little ball of fluff. The dog always calmed her nerves.

She went down the line of everything she knew about horse health in the final months of pregnancy. No clear diagnosis came to mind based on what Marc had told her. She'd have to wait to see for herself.

When she arrived at his ranch, he waved her to the stables. She wasted no time parking and grabbing her supplies. Marc explained the situation in more detail as she zipped up her lightweight coveralls.

"She's in the paddock over here." Marc unlocked the gate, waited for her to enter, followed her inside and closed it once more.

The pretty mahogany quarter horse had a white diamond on her forehead, and her forelegs, mane and tail were black. She raised her head as they approached. She had a listless air about her.

"Hey there, Miss Lightning." Mackenzie used her soothing voice as she slowly approached the mare. The horse looked to be a healthy weight. She took her temperature, listened to her lungs and performed an overall health check.

The stethoscope hung around her neck as she continued to study Miss Lightning. The weather hadn't been scorching hot, nor did there seem to be any infection or typical problem a pregnant mare might face.

What was she missing?

"She hasn't been eating fescue?" she asked.

"No, she hasn't."

"Is she up-to-date on her vaccines?"

"I'm not sure. Dr. Banks came out regularly until he retired..." Marc rubbed the back of his neck.

"I understand."

"I have her records. I can get them."

"That would be a big help." As Marc loped away, Mackenzie stroked the horse's neck, murmuring sweet nothings to her.

Then she examined her front legs and hooves—and immediately recognized what was wrong. Marc strode back with a folder in his hand.

"When was the last time her hooves were trimmed?"

"It hasn't been too long...wait...when did I have it done?" His eyes grew round as he nodded. "Of course. It's been a good six months. I could kick myself. I'm always on top of everything, but we had her shoes taken off in the winter since we weren't riding her. Normally, Doctor Banks would remind me about her hooves."

"It's okay. I can take care of it now. She's still far enough away from her due date that it shouldn't cause a problem, and it will make her more comfortable as the foal grows bigger."

They discussed the particulars, and Mackenzie backed the trailer up to the paddock. She'd known the extra expense of the portable hydraulic lift would be worth it. This little mama would be as comfortable as Mackenzie could make her while she took care of those hooves.

When it was over, Marc took the horse back into the paddock while Mackenzie removed her suit and locked the trailer.

Three women and two toddler girls strode their way across the lawn.

"Mackenzie, have you met my wife, Reagan?" Marc walked back to her as the ladies arrived.

"No, but I hear you make the best chocolates around."

"That's very kind." Reagan had a quiet air about her. "What's your favorite? I'll make you a batch. We appreciate you coming out to help Miss Lightning."

"I'm happy to do it. But I'm not turning down sweets. I love chocolate-covered pretzels."

"Dark or milk chocolate?"

"Milk."

"Done." Reagan beamed and turned to the middle-aged woman Mackenzie had chatted with several times at the bakery. "This is Anne, Marc's mom, and Brooke, his sister. And these two little sweeties are Alice and Megan."

"Oh! They're identical." What adorable little girls. Both had dark curls, big blue eyes and chubby cheeks.

"Is Miss Lightning going to be okay?" Brooke couldn't hide the worry in her eyes.

"She'll be fine. Her hooves needed trimming. If she still seems off over the next couple of days, call me. I'll come out and check on her."

"What a relief." Brooke's face cleared, then scrunched in disgust when she checked on the twins. "Alice, put down that worm!"

Mackenzie stuck around for a few minutes before saying goodbye. Later, as she drove back to town, she said a silent prayer. *God, thank You for giving me the wisdom to know what was wrong with Miss Lightning. Thank You for reminding me You're with me at all times. I can depend on You.*

She hadn't panicked. She'd been fine. And spending time chatting with Marc's family had made her feel welcome and appreciated. Maybe Dad was on to something about making a life here. And now that Cade had asked her out on an actual date, maybe it wouldn't be as hard as she thought.

What if he wanted to get serious, though?

She gripped the steering wheel. One date did not automatically lead to wedding bells. She'd keep it casual. As much as she liked Cade's company, she wasn't sure she was capable of getting close to him. He might only be asking her to tour the stables for his own reasons. She couldn't count on keeping his interest long-term. But, for once, she wished she could. A guy like Cade didn't come around all that often.

Chapter Eight

Excitement added a spring to his step the next morning, and it wasn't anticipation of the Fourth of July fireworks that night. Cade strode down the main aisle of the stables with a box of doughnuts in one hand and a cardboard caddy holding two iced coffees in the other. Tulip kept her nose to the ground as she trotted ahead of him. Mackenzie would be arriving in fifteen minutes. He was eager to find out what she thought of his property.

Yesterday afternoon, Cade had driven to Ty's house and asked him if he could think of anyone qualified to manage Moulten Stables. After discussing the options, Ty had snapped his fingers and announced, "Trent Lloyd."

Trent had graduated from high school with Ty and moved away for college. Ty talked to him occasionally and believed he'd graduated with an equine degree in Alabama. After Cade left Ty's, he called and left a message for Trent. If he wasn't the right person for the job, he'd have to post the position online and hope for the best.

Discussing Moulten Stables with Ty had helped Cade lighten up about offering perfection to Forestline Adventures. He didn't need to beg any company to board their horses with him. He was offering a high-end service that had few true competitors. Yes, there were plenty of horse-boarding operations around the state, but none had the facilities and attention to detail his would.

Tulip sniffed her way to the makeshift office, and Cade set the doughnuts and coffees on the table. Then he bent to pet the dog.

"You're going to visit the nursing home next week." He used his baby-talk voice and chuckled as her little tongue panted in a smile. "You've almost got it down on how to avoid the wheelchair. Pretty soon, you'll be coming with me and Mom every time we visit Nana. You'll like that, won't you?"

He stopped petting her, and she pranced in place until he picked her up. Cuddling her to his chest, he kept stroking her fur.

"Charlene is going to love you. I guarantee she'll keep a box of treats for you at her station."

Tulip let out a yip, and he laughed, setting her on the ground. "I hear you. I like treats, too."

"Knock, knock." Mackenzie stood in the doorway.

Cade sucked in a breath and held it. Talk about a treat. What was it about her that stirred his emotions? Her hair hung over her shoulder in a long braid, and she wore a short-sleeved blouse with shorts and sandals. She was as beautiful as a meadow full of spring flowers.

Mackenzie approached and, smiling, picked up the dog. "Hello, sweet Tulip."

He took one of the coffees and waited for her to set the dog down before he handed it to her.

"Thank you. So this is it, huh?" Her eyes sparkled, and he wanted to reach out and touch her hand, but he held back. Wasn't his place. Her gaze fell beyond him. "Ooh, are those the doughnuts you promised?"

"Yes, help yourself."

"Don't mind if I do." She set her coffee on the table, then

flipped open the lid of the box and took her time selecting one. She ended up with a cruller. No shock there. "Is it okay if I sit?"

"Go ahead." Cade reached past her to grab a chocolate-covered doughnut as she took a seat. He sat in the chair next to her, angling his to see her better. His doughnut went down in three bites.

"I didn't realize you had so much property." Mackenzie took a sip of her iced coffee.

"Twenty acres." He began to relax, remembering when he'd first bought the land not long after Dad passed away. Even then, he'd figured it would be a good investment. It had taken a few years for him to know what to do with it, and now his plan was almost in place.

"Why horses?" She took another bite of her doughnut, and he briefly considered snagging a second one for himself. Yeah, why not? He took a cruller out of the box.

"I was talking to a buddy from my days on Wall Street, and he told me he'd rented a cabin up in the Big Horn Mountains for a week. Apparently, his group went big-game hunting. They rode horses, went trout fishing and raved about how great it was to get away from it all."

"Sounds like an active vacation."

"Yeah, well, they had a chef on-site, a housekeeper and plenty of downtime." He chuckled. "And when I say cabin, I mean massive log home with all the amenities."

She brushed crumbs from her hands. "My kind of cabin."

"Luxury has its perks." He nodded to her iced coffee. "Want to walk and talk?"

"Sure. By the way, everyone's talking about the tour you gave Paris." She picked up her coffee and stood, batting her eyelashes at him. "Greta got all the updates from our clients, including the Instagram picture of you two together that I'm told went viral. I have to say, she's as stunning as they all said."

"She's not my type."

"She's every guy's type."

"Not mine."

"Okay, then what is your type?"

"Not her."

They made their way to the doorway leading to the rest of the stables.

"Did the meeting go well?" she asked. "Did she give you any indication their company wants to board their horses with you?"

"It went well. She didn't make any promises, but none of her concerns were deal-breakers, either. I wish the place was finished. Then she could have seen for herself the final product."

"Eh, that's just cosmetics. I'm sure she saw beyond the construction zone. You have a lot to offer them."

"I hope you're right, but I don't know. Cosmetics tend to seal the deal." He shrugged. "I'm letting Tulip off-leash here if that's okay. All work and no play…"

"I approve."

Cade waited for Mackenzie to exit the office, and Tulip darted ahead of them. "Anyway, back to my buddy. I started thinking about the horses and who took care of them during the off-season. I did some research into the types of luxury vacation services people like him use and found out they board their horses during the winter. After I talked to a few of the managers, I realized the disadvantage they have by boarding the horses themselves."

"You saw a need, and you're filling it." Mackenzie matched his easy strides.

"Exactly." He stopped when they reached the main aisle.

"I'm surprised." She looked up at him, the cup dangling

from her hand. "I was sure you were going to tell me how much you love horses."

He frowned. Should he have answered differently? "I do love horses."

"But?"

"But I'm a businessman. I make decisions based on profitability."

"I see." She turned away to check on Tulip. The dog moseyed into one of the recently built stalls.

Did she have a problem with him making money? Or was he reading into things? Getting defensive because of his past?

"From what I see, this should be profitable. What's going on there?" She pointed to the caution tape he'd extended last night from one stall across the aisle to the opposite stall. Paris's comment had him toying with ideas—one of which was to divide the barn in half. That way the locals' horses would be separate from his other clients' horses. But was it really necessary?

"It came to my attention that the companies trusting me with their expensive, well-trained horses might not want the general public mingling with them."

"What do you mean?"

Tulip came out of the stall with her head high and joined them. They resumed their stroll.

"I'm offering stalls at a discount for locals to board their horses here. I also plan on keeping a handful of horses onsite to rent to the high-school kids who want to join the rodeo team but don't have the funds to buy one of their own. Ty and I talked about it last night, and he's going to help me start buying suitable horses."

"Won't that cut into your profits?" she asked with a teasing smile.

"No. Actually, it's the reason I'm going after the luxury market. If I can take care of their horses, it will bring in enough income to fund the entire operation and allow me to offer low prices to the teens."

"Hmm." With a soft smile, she paused near the caution tape. "I can't figure you out."

"What do you mean?" He got an uneasy feeling. Like when his dad had visited him in New York. Was Mackenzie about to call him out on something? But what?

"I don't know. On the one hand, you're a successful rancher and businessman. On the other hand, you seem to have time to help everyone. And then there's this." She extended her arm to the barn. "It's just… I don't get you."

"Get me? What is there to get?"

She used her iced coffee to point to the caution tape. "You're like that tape. One side is catering to wealthy people, and the other is helping the community."

"Is that bad?"

"Of course not." She shook her head. "I'm just not sure where you fit. Are you in the middle? On one side? Or the other?"

A reply in his defense leaped to his tongue, but he swallowed it.

She'd hit on something. He'd been trying to figure out how and where he fit, too. He'd been trying for years. And as far as the community, he'd always been a part of it. As much as he wanted to tell her he didn't fit in with the wealthy clients, it would be a lie. He couldn't deny he was still drawn to their world, and their opinion of him mattered.

But then again, he had acquaintances from his time in the city, but he wasn't close to any of them. That, too, had to mean something. He wasn't sure what. He hadn't embraced being a cowboy, either. He still wanted his investments. Still constantly searched for his next venture.

He chalked it up to his restless nature. But maybe it was more.

Today wasn't the time to think about it. Today was for hanging out with Mackenzie.

"Come on. I'll show you the rest of the property."

For the next hour, Cade gave her a thorough tour. He answered her questions about the materials he'd selected and showed her the same digital rendering he'd shown Paris depicting the stalls, the tack room, the bathrooms and the common area.

"Cade?" she asked as they finished walking along one of the new riding paths.

"Yes?"

"Why are you showing me all this?"

Because I want to. Why else would he show her around? He enjoyed having her here. Liked telling her about his plans. The fact that she was interested in what he had to say filled a neglected part of him—a lonely side of him.

"I thought you'd like to see it."

"You're not going to try to talk me into becoming the full-time vet for this place, are you?" Her tone was light, but it held an edge of truth.

Ahh…he'd forgotten about that. How, in a few short weeks, had he gone from wanting an equine-certified vet to merely enjoying her company?

"No," he said, forcing a grin, "but if you want to get certified in equine care, I wouldn't complain."

"You never give up, do you?" Her eyes sparkled as she grinned. "You do know it takes six years of experience, usually with a residency, to qualify for certification, don't you?"

No, he did not know that. "I take it that means you're not interested in going that route."

"Correct." She headed to where the arena had been cleared.

The sun gleamed on her braid, and he couldn't help admiring everything about her.

"You'll still be on call for my horses, right?"

"Of course. You can count on me."

As he took in her profile, it hit him that he could count on her and not just for vet services. He'd seen her in action. Had faith in her abilities as a veterinarian. But he also liked being in her company. He found himself wanting to tell her things he didn't feel comfortable sharing with other people.

By the time they finished discussing the outdoor arena, Tulip was panting from the climbing temperatures. Mackenzie gazed off to the edge of his property.

"I should probably get her out of the sun," Cade said. "Is your dad coming to the festival? I should have told you to bring him."

"Nope. I told him about it, but he said he wants to work with Charger, the German shepherd he recently adopted. By the way, he's been talking with contractors about getting the training center renovated."

"That's good news. I'm sure he's excited to get started."

"Yes, he is." Mackenzie wiped the back of her neck. "Whew. It's getting hot."

"Let's head back. It's time to have some fun." Cade picked up Tulip as they made their way back to the stables.

"What kind of fun are we talking about?" she asked.

"We're talking shaved ices, fresh-cut french fries, live music and kids waving American flags. If Mary Corning is involved, there will be a kettle-corn booth set up in the park."

"I love kettle corn."

"I do, too. Oh, and fireworks."

"Can't have the Fourth of July without those."

"Right?"

"Okay, cowboy. I'm ready. Let's get patriotic."

Cade grinned. He liked the sound of that. "I have to drop off Tulip and pick up Mom. Want to join me?"

"Will she read too much into it if I'm with you?" Mackenzie's worried expression cracked him up.

"Absolutely." He nodded. "She reads too much into everything if it involves me or my brother being around a woman."

"Maybe it's time for me to live a little dangerously."

"You're really living on the wild side."

"Tell me about it."

They looked at each other and smiled. Why did he have the feeling *he* was the one living dangerously? And why was his heart pounding *yes, yes, yes*?

"I guess we aren't living dangerously after all." Mackenzie finished setting up the crate and small dog bed in her living room fifteen minutes later. Christy had called Cade as they were heading to their trucks at his stables. Apparently, one of her friends had picked her up for the festival. Instead of driving all the way to his ranch, Mackenzie had suggested letting Tulip stay at her house while they walked around town. The dog was used to being there.

"What should I use for a water bowl?" Cade called from the kitchen on the other side of the hallway that ran down the center of the one-story home.

"I have bowls for her. I'll get them." She fluffed the bed, and Tulip hopped onto it, then circled around twice before curling up for a nap. Mackenzie gently petted her before heading to the kitchen.

She brushed past Cade, all too aware of the fresh scent of his cologne. The dog bowls were stacked in a lower cupboard. She filled one with water and made her way to the back of the house, where her laundry room was located. She always kept cat food and dog food on hand in case someone found a stray or an injured animal and needed her to keep it for the night.

Back in the kitchen, she set the bowl with the dog food next to the water bowl, then looked around to see if she was missing anything for little Tulip. She didn't think so.

"Are you ready?" she asked.

"I am. Let me say goodbye to Tulip first." He went into the living room, crouched next to the dog bed, murmured something Mackenzie couldn't make out and petted her. The dog licked her lips and closed her eyes again. "I think this morning tired her out."

"I think you're right."

When they got to the driveway, Cade motioned to keep going. "You're close to town. It's always hard to find a parking spot since Center Street gets blocked off. Why don't we walk?"

"Sounds good to me."

They fell in step next to each other on the sidewalk.

"Have you heard from your mother since she called?" Cade asked.

"We talked the night of the grand opening, but we haven't spoken since." It was a relief. For over a week now, she'd been half expecting her mother to pull into her driveway. The more time that passed, the more she loosened up. If Mom hadn't shown up by now, there was a good chance she wouldn't at all.

"The conversation didn't go well?" He continued at a pace she had no problem matching.

"She threatened to come visit."

"Threatened?" He chuckled, glanced her way and sobered. "Oh, you're serious."

"Dead serious. I used to enjoy her visits. I'd get so excited to find her on my doorstep."

"What happened to change it?"

What happened? Mackenzie had finally opened her eyes to reality, that was what happened.

"She's good at pretending she's here to see me, but there's always another reason—a selfish one—for an impromptu visit. That's what she does. She lulls you into thinking she cares, and you help her. Then she takes off without a warning. You don't see or hear from her for months, even years."

"I didn't realize..."

Although he sounded like he could possibly understand, she doubted he did. Look at his family—his mom was everything Mackenzie's mom wasn't. Christy was generous and thoughtful. Her gift for the clinic's opening still touched Mackenzie's heart. The tall black planters with red geraniums, white petunias and green ivy made the entrance to the clinic so much more inviting than anything Mackenzie would have come up with on her own. And this from someone she'd barely known at the time.

Her mother, on the other hand, wouldn't think to bring a gift to celebrate her grand opening. Mackenzie couldn't remember the last time her mom had called to wish her a happy birthday or had sent her a Christmas gift. She didn't need or expect gifts, but she did want her mother to at least care about her.

Maybe that was what hurt. Knowing her own mother didn't really love her. Every word the woman spoke was meaningless. Empty. Bonnie might insist on spending time together when she showed up, but it wasn't out of love. She always had an ulterior motive.

"Do you think she'll actually come to Jewel River?" Cade asked.

"I hope not." Mackenzie kept her gaze ahead. "I have no idea, though. If she does, I don't know how long she'd stay. A week? A month? Who knows? She's not bunking with me."

She glanced his way and wished she hadn't. Cade was handsome on a whole different level. And she was a no-frills, busy, single woman in her thirties.

Friends. They were friends.

On a date.

Did that make them more than friends?

Could she handle being more? Could he?

It wasn't only the time issue—all of the after-hours emergencies and being on call she anticipated dealing with soon. Cade was respected and well-liked and involved with the community. She wasn't used to having a social life, and she wasn't sure she wanted one. But, out of everyone she'd met over the past several years, she felt the most comfortable with Cade. And what about last night? She'd enjoyed talking to Reagan, Marc and Brooke.

Stop worrying about the future. Just enjoy today.

They turned the corner and soon joined the crowds on Center Street, where the smells of barbecue, popcorn and funnel cakes mingled in the air. Country music blared through speakers mounted on a makeshift stage. Everywhere she looked, people of all ages were enjoying themselves. Some were in line at the food trucks. Others ambled around the craft booths. Laughing teens weaved their way through the crowd.

"I had no idea it would be this busy." She slowed to get her bearings.

"Cade!" A trio of women headed their way. Mackenzie recognized all three—Erica, Reagan and Brooke. Another woman—a curvy blonde—ran up to Brooke and hugged her.

"Hello, ladies." Cade had a spark of mischief in his eyes. "What food truck should we start with?"

"Mackenzie, I didn't see you there." Erica came right up to Mackenzie and hugged her. Then she stepped back and glanced at the other women. "You've met Reagan and Brooke, right?"

"Yes, we met last night." Mackenzie turned to Reagan. "How is Miss Lightning?"

"Great. She's acting like herself again. I'm so glad you were around to help. Marc is relieved. He's mad at himself for missing the signs."

"What happened to Miss Lightning?" Cade asked.

"I trimmed her hooves." Mackenzie shrugged as if it was nothing. Because it wasn't a big deal. She'd feared the worst and been blessed with an easy fix.

Brooke stepped forward with her friend. "Mackenzie, this is my best friend, Gracie French. I keep trying to convince her to move back here, but she won't listen." Brooke grinned, clearly teasing.

Gracie elbowed Brooke's side. "You never know. Stranger things have happened."

"Let's make it happen," Brooke said. "I miss you. It's always better when you're around."

"We'd better scoot," Erica said with an apologetic smile. "Dalton and Marc have their hands full with the kids over at the cotton-candy booth." She reached over and gave Mackenzie's arm a light squeeze. "It was great running into you. We need to get together soon. Hang out. Have a coffee at Annie's Bakery or something."

The thoughtful gesture went straight to Mackenzie's heart. The people of Jewel River made her feel right at home. All those times she'd told herself she didn't have time for friendships or relationships—had she been lying to herself?

Maybe she'd always had time for friends but hadn't made it a priority. Surely, she could fit in a coffee date with Erica or any of the women she'd recently met. They all seemed down-to-earth and fun.

If she could make time for a friend or two, she could probably make time for a boyfriend as well. What if time wasn't the issue at all?

"Oh, boy." Cade took Mackenzie by the arm. "Quick, let's go to the barbecue truck."

"Why?" She forced herself to hurry as he broke into a light jog.

"My mother, Mary Corning and Charlene Parker are up ahead buying candles. They haven't spotted us yet. We still have time to escape."

She had to hustle to keep up with him. "Why are we running?"

He gave her a sideways glance and didn't slow a bit. "Are you prepared for questions—and I mean terrible questions—from them?"

"How terrible?" Slightly out of breath, she scrunched her nose.

"The worst. It will start with them cooing over you."

Cooing? "As in a dove?"

"Yes." He stopped next to a table with condiments and napkins. Tugged her beside him to hide behind the line of people waiting for barbecue pulled pork. Then he craned his neck this way and that before staring directly into her eyes. "After the cooing, the questions will begin. It will seem innocent, but trust me, it's not."

He altered his tone to sound like his mother. "How are you settling in? Did you know we have a book club on Thursdays? Oh, Cade, you should bring her to book club. I have a novel for you, Mackenzie. It's a romance. Love at first sight. You'll adore it. Do you ever think about getting married? I've always thought a summer wedding is the way to go. The Winston is the best venue. And Dorothy Bell does the most beautiful flower arrangements."

Mackenzie couldn't contain her laughter any longer, and she guffawed. A few people in line turned at the noise. Sheepishly, she covered her mouth but continued to giggle softly.

"You laugh, but it gets worse." His eyes had a panicked gleam, and he looked over her head and groaned. "I knew we should have hidden behind the building. They spotted us."

Mackenzie turned as Christy, Mary and Charlene pushed through the crowd to stand in front of them. The three women were all smiles.

"I didn't expect to see you two here," Christy said, her grin wider than the Grand Canyon, as she gave Mackenzie a hug. Two hugs in one day. Huh. "Cade, that was so thoughtful of you to bring her to the festival. I was going to suggest it, but I got busy and forgot."

"Yes, it's sure good to see you kids getting out and about." Mary nodded. "This'll give you a chance to get to know each other better. I say a little barbecue, an ice cream cone and a blanket at the fireworks is a real good way to spend your time."

Mackenzie didn't dare look at Cade. She was afraid she'd burst out laughing again.

"Now, Mackenzie, are you settling in okay, hon?" Charlene had a concerned look. "You know we have a book club, right?"

A book club? She'd thought Cade had been kidding.

"That's a great idea!" Christy piped up, nodding rapidly. "Cade, you should bring Mackenzie to the book club. That way she won't feel awkward." Christy turned her attention back to her. "I know it's uncomfortable walking into a room where you don't know anyone."

"Do you still have the book from April, Christy?" Charlene steepled her fingers. "That was a goodie."

Christy brightened. "Why yes, I do, Char. Mackenzie, I

think you'll like this one. It's a reunion romance. There's a secret baby involved, but don't let that throw you off."

Mackenzie found herself speechless. How had Cade known?

"Cade, honey," Charlene said, reaching out to pat his arm. "I'll make sure Janey sends you an invitation to the wedding that says *plus one* on it. That way you can bring Mackenzie with you."

"Perfect," Christy said, nodding.

"That is really thoughtful of you, Charlene." Cade stared at something beyond the women and pointed. "Hey? Is that Clem? I'll wave him over."

The women's smiles vanished, and they shared a long, serious look. His mother was the first to speak. "We'll let you two get on with your day." She leaned in toward Mackenzie. "Be sure to go to the booth at the end. Laura is having a buy-one-get-one sale on her candles."

"We'll do that."

"Oh, good, he's almost here." Cade's tone was innocent. "I don't want you ladies to miss him."

"No, no. We'll find him later." The women scurried away.

Mary called over her shoulder, "Go get yourselves some kettle corn, kids."

"We will!" Cade yelled.

Mackenzie scanned the people in the area. "I don't see Clem."

"That's because he's not there." Cade grinned. "You can thank me later."

She shook her head as she chuckled. "You're terrible."

"Am I? I think you meant to say I'm your hero." He grabbed her hand and herded her around a young couple pushing a stroller. "I saved you from the next phase of questions. You were about to get bombarded with the do-you-like-kids question. That would be followed up with 'How soon do you see yourself with a family?' Trust me, I did the right thing."

Mackenzie's mood soared like the red, white and blue balloons bobbing in clusters up and down the street. Cade was fun to be with. It didn't escape her notice that he hadn't let go of her hand, either. If he wanted to get his mother and her friends off his back about them as a couple, he had a weird way of showing it.

Maybe he didn't want them off his back. He was the one who'd said this was a date, right?

Why, though? Why would handsome, successful, popular Cade Moulten be interested in her?

Stop it! This was her day off, and she was going to enjoy it. Even if it meant holding Cade's hand. Especially if it meant holding Cade's hand.

For the next couple of hours, they made their way through every craft booth. They bought lunch and snacks and shaved ices. Everywhere they went, people stopped to talk to Cade. He introduced her to them, and he took special care to point out to the ranchers that she was the new veterinarian.

They were on their way back to Mackenzie's house to check on Tulip when Mackenzie came to a halt on the sidewalk. Couldn't move if she tried.

Her mother was walking straight toward them. And Dad was with her.

Mackenzie swallowed the bitter taste in her mouth.

"What's wrong?" Cade frowned down at her.

Squaring her shoulders, she widened her stance and kept her gaze on her parents.

"My mother's in town."

"She is?" He followed her gaze. "Is she the one with your dad?"

"Yes."

As soon as they neared, her mom threw her arms around Mackenzie. She stood there like a statue until her mother stepped back.

Cade greeted her father, who introduced her to Bonnie. After they exchanged pleasantries, no one seemed to know what else to say.

"What are you doing here?" Mackenzie didn't want to sound so mean, but really? On today of all days, her mom had to show up?

"I told you I missed you." Mom had her pretending-to-care face on. Too bad it was a mask. Easily slipped on and off.

Mackenzie faced her dad. "What are you doing together?"

"Just thought we'd see what the festival was all about." His eyes were full of understanding, yet Mackenzie didn't think he understood at all.

"Don't worry. I'm not staying with you." Her mother's tone was getting under her skin. "Patrick said I can stay with him."

She circled her fingers over her temples. Why was this happening? Why now? Why here?

"How long will you be in town?" She tried—really tried—to sound pleasant.

"Oh, I don't know." Mom shrugged happily.

"Not long." Dad crinkled his nose.

No one spoke. The sounds of laughter and music in the distance made the silence more pronounced.

"We have to go check on Tulip." Mackenzie jerked her thumb to the right.

"Go, go." Mom waved the backs of her fingers in a fluttery manner. "We'll catch up soon."

She didn't respond. Just marched away. Cade said goodbye to them and hurried to join her.

It had been a near-perfect day. She should have known her mother would ruin it.

The woman ruined everything.

"Do you want to talk about it?" Cade kept a brisk pace next to Mackenzie as they turned the corner of her street.

"No."

The only time he'd seen Mackenzie like this—pale, tense, jittery with anger—had been when her mom called during the grand opening.

"Your parents seem to get along, huh?"

"Not really." She flicked him a glance. "They don't have much contact with each other."

"Hmm." Her house was up ahead. American flags waved from the neighboring porches, and most of the lawns had yellow patches from the lack of rain.

"What?"

"Why is she staying with him?" He found it strange. Were her parents reconnecting or something?

"Because I point-blank told her she couldn't stay with me."

He kept his mouth shut until they climbed her porch steps. She opened the door, and he held it for her to go inside. She zoomed straight to Tulip, who must have heard them and was waiting in the hallway, wagging her tail.

"Were you a good girl?" Mackenzie gathered the pup in her arms and petted her. "Did you have a nice nap?"

They went through the kitchen and out to the backyard. Cade stayed behind. In no time at all, Mackenzie and Tulip were back inside. She carried the dog to the living room and sat on the couch. Cade crammed next to her. On her lap, Tulip nudged her hand. Mackenzie's rigid stance slowly melted as she caressed the dog's fur.

Cade wanted to comfort her, too, but he wasn't sure how.

Her mother had seemed nice enough. Pleasant, anyway. Looks could be deceiving, though.

"My mother is what I guess you'd call a free spirit." She kept her gaze on Tulip's fur. Her throat worked as she swallowed. "I don't know what she's looking for, but it's not me."

"She found you here, though."

A brittle laugh erupted from her. "Yes, she always finds me. But only when she's desperate and needs something."

"Like what?"

"A place to stay until she can cook up her next adventure and get the money—from me—to fund it."

Oh. He grimaced. That didn't sound good.

"The sad thing, though, is if things were different, I'd love for her to stay with me more often. I actually like hearing her figure out her next job and where she'll move. I never minded giving her money to help her get started."

"But?" He took her hand in his, and she didn't pull it away.

"But that's all I am to her. A couch to crash on. A wallet to borrow from. Then she's out the door and out of my life."

Indignation began to spread in his chest.

"She's dishonest. She pretends to be someone she's not. And it hurts, Cade. After last time, I told myself I wasn't falling for her act again. I can't. I won't."

He wrapped his arms around her, with Tulip between them, and held her. She softened in his embrace, and he wanted to tell her he'd never let anyone hurt her again. But how could he?

She was the first to pull back. "I don't expect you to understand. Your family is close and loving."

Yeah, they were. But that didn't mean he couldn't understand the whole pretending-to-be-someone-you're-not situation.

Hadn't he done the same thing?

Wasn't he still doing the same thing?

"Hopefully," Mackenzie said, "she'll get restless and move on quickly."

Restless.

He knew all about getting restless, too. A sour taste bloomed in his mouth.

"I can't trust her, and I'm tired of trying." Mackenzie looked so vulnerable. He wanted to kiss her and make her forget about her pain.

But he didn't. He couldn't.

Mackenzie didn't deserve to be hurt. She thought he was someone he wasn't. Thought he was respectable—a stand-up guy.

He'd gotten his hands dirty. And nothing he could say or do would ever change it. He wouldn't burden her with the details.

Burden her? Come on. Don't lie to yourself. You hide it because you're embarrassed. Ashamed.

"I'm not in the mood to go back to the festival," Mackenzie said. "I hope you don't mind."

"I understand. We can still watch the fireworks from your backyard."

"Really?" Her eyes lit up with hope.

"Yeah." He put his arm around her shoulders and drew her closer to lean on him. He kissed the side of her head. "We'll stay right here."

And after tonight, he needed to do a better job of keeping his distance. She'd been hurt enough. Getting close would only add to her pain.

Chapter Nine

Working with Tulip at the clinic was one thing. Working with her at the nursing home was another. Would the dog get nervous and forget her training?

Cade squashed his worries as he held open the door to the nursing home for his mother the following Tuesday afternoon. Wearing her therapy-dog vest, Tulip walked beside Christy with slack in her leash the way Mackenzie expected. The dog rarely strained at the leash anymore on their nightly walks, and she no longer viewed the wheelchair as a threat, either.

Up ahead, Mackenzie chatted with Charlene, and when she spotted them, she excused herself and strolled their way. His mother stopped in front of Mackenzie. Tulip sat at Mom's feet. Cade joined them, keeping his eye on the dog, but she seemed content where she was, smiling up at Mackenzie.

Maybe this session would go better than he feared.

He didn't know why he was worried. This was a practice run—a training session. It wouldn't count against Tulip if she struggled, failed to obey commands or barked like she had last week with the wheelchair.

Cade just wanted her to pass her test. Wanted Nana to enjoy the dog—while she still could.

After the fireworks, he'd tried hard to put Mackenzie out of his mind, but she was wedged in there. Keeping a friendly distance? Forget it. He'd texted her every day about her mom (she'd been avoiding her), the ranches she was visiting (none since the Fourth), how Charger was settling in (great) and if she wanted the romance novel his mom recommended (a hard pass on that one).

Over the weekend, Ty had told him about a few horses for sale, and Cade had taken one look at the black Morgan horse named Licorice and had known she would be perfect for Mackenzie. He and Ty had contacted the owner and driven out there on Sunday to inspect the beauty. Cade had purchased Licorice, and Ty had bought the other horse for sale.

Since Mackenzie didn't have time to take care of her own horse, Cade figured he'd provide one for her. Licorice would stay on his ranch until the new facility opened. Then he'd have his staff take care of her along with the other horses. Mackenzie could stop by Moulten Stables and ride her whenever her heart desired. No strings attached.

He'd been thinking a lot about her heart and its desires lately. Thinking about his own, too.

Ty was picking up both horses and bringing Licorice to his ranch tomorrow morning. It was perfect timing, since Cade had spent an hour with Trent Lloyd on the phone about the manager position, and Trent would also be arriving tomorrow to check out the stables and interview for the job. His credentials were impressive, and the fact he'd grown up around here made him the ideal candidate. But Cade really wanted to see him interact with Licorice.

"Where's Patrick?" Mom asked Mackenzie as she looked around the reception area.

"He'll be here."

"Is your mother coming, too?"

Cade should have warned his mom not to bring up her mother.

"I have no idea." She didn't seem upset.

"Oh, before we get started, I have something for you." Christy dug around in her large purse, then pulled out a paperback. Her smile could only be described as triumphant. "The book I mentioned. Book club isn't for two more weeks, and I can get you a copy of this month's selection if you want to join us."

A frown line appeared as Mackenzie studied the cover of a woman holding a baby. "I don't know. This isn't really my thing." She tried to hand it back to his mother, but Mom just shook her head and pushed the book back to Mackenzie.

"You'll love it. Trust me. Keep it."

Patrick entered the building and headed straight to them. He was alone. Probably for the best.

"I'm going to be observing and taking notes, so ignore me." Patrick nodded in greeting to them as he pulled out a clipboard.

"Let's begin." Mackenzie addressed his mom. "Christy, why don't you give Charlene your purse? Cade, would you go down to the end of that hall and set up a trail of treats like we did at the clinic last week?"

He didn't have to be told twice. The reception area was the central hub of the nursing home, and three wings branched off from it. One led to the dining hall and activities center. The other two housed the residents. Both of those wings ended in circular common areas surrounded by windows.

Cade headed down the closest hall and placed treats a few feet apart on the floor at the end. Then he straightened and gazed out the windows. Birdfeeders and benches had been installed in the fenced-in back lawn. The view was peaceful. He'd have to bring Nana down here on one of her good days.

He returned to the reception desk. Several staff members were oohing and ahhing over Tulip, and she smiled at them with her tongue out as she continued to sit quietly by his mom's side. A rush of pride filled his chest.

The dog—their dog—was behaving the way they'd trained her.

When the meet and greet ended, Mackenzie asked Charlene and one of the nurse's aides if it would be possible to bring a few residents down the hall past Tulip.

"Sure thing, hon." Charlene grinned. "They're about done with their afternoon snack."

Mackenzie instructed him and his mother on how they should handle Tulip. Soon, a man in a wheelchair emerged from the activities room and wheeled himself down the hall toward them. Tulip stayed calm. Then an aide helped a woman with her walker.

Cade tensed as he watched the dog. How would she handle this? Two people *and* a walker. Tulip looked up at Christy, and she simply smiled and reminded her to sit, praising her for obeying as they approached. After they passed by, Mom gave Tulip a treat.

Another woman with a walker approached.

"Hi, Dolores," Mom said to the woman. "What activity did you do today?"

"Heh?" Dolores Jones squinted.

"Activity," Mom said loudly. "What did you do today?"

"I didn't want to color, so I didn't."

"Maybe next time."

Dolores noticed Tulip. "What's that?"

"It's my dog, Tulip. She's going to be coming around to visit soon. She's in training."

Her face softened, and she wiggled her fingers to Tulip. "Hey there, puppy."

Tulip wagged her tail but didn't move.

After a steady line of residents trickled past from the activities center to their rooms, Mackenzie and Patrick agreed it would be a good time to move to the end of the hall, where Cade had placed the treats.

"Cade, why don't you take the lead on this?" Mom handed him the leash.

"Okay." He didn't want to take the lead. Not with half the staff watching and Mackenzie's dad taking notes. But he'd pull up his big-boy pants and do it.

"Remember what to do?" Mackenzie asked.

"I tell her to leave it, and I lead her past each treat." They'd practiced this for a few weeks. They'd started by giving her an even better treat each time she ignored one on the floor, and they'd worked up to rewarding her with a special chew bone if she left all the treats with only one command.

"Right. Go on and move to the back. I'll tell you when to start." As soon as he and Tulip were ready, she gave them the go-ahead.

"Leave it." He walked Tulip past the treats. She didn't even sniff them.

"Okay, now weave your way back."

He did, and again, she ignored all the little treats on the floor. When they finished, he crouched and ruffled her fur. "Good job. You did amazing."

Cade handed her a small chew bone.

"What do you think, Dad?" Mackenzie tilted her head to Patrick. "Anything else you want to see?"

"Not today. She's done well." Patrick motioned for Christy and Cade to come closer. "If you want to practice her meeting other dogs, we can set up a time with Charger. I've been working with him, and he's learned to stay calm and not run over to other dogs or their owners."

"Yes, we'll do that," Christy said. "We've taken her to town a few times, and she's done a pretty good job of ignoring the other dogs…"

Cade kept an eye on Tulip, still munching on her treat, and sidled up next to Mackenzie. "Do you think there's any way I could take Tulip to meet Nana right now?"

"Normally, I would say yes. But Tulip has dealt with a lot of new things today, and I don't want to overwhelm her." Her deep blue eyes were bright. "It's not that I don't think Tulip is ready."

"I understand." He did. Kind of. "I'm going to pop down there and say hi."

"I'll come with you."

While he liked the thought of Mackenzie with him, he didn't want her to be freaked out if Nana thought he was his father or said something else that was weird. "Nana isn't always with it. Sometimes she thinks I'm someone else."

"Don't worry about it." She patted his arm. "I understand."

"Ma, we're going to say hi to Nana for a minute." He handed her Tulip's leash.

"Okay, Cade." Mom smiled. "I'll stay here with our princess until you're done."

Cade's grandmother had been sleeping, but the tenderness in the way he held the woman's hand as she slept had tugged at Mackenzie's heart. She understood at a deeper level why he and Christy were so adamant about getting Tulip certified.

They wanted to bring a little joy into his grandmother's life. Who could argue with that?

Standing next to her father in the nursing home's parking lot, Mackenzie waved goodbye to Cade, Christy and Tulip. Then she turned to her dad. "I'm taking off, too."

Normally, she would ask him to have supper with her, but with her mom still around, Mackenzie couldn't stomach it.

"Wait," he said.

She paused next to her truck.

"The three of us need to talk."

The three of us? They hadn't been a trio for two decades. Why start now?

"No, thank you."

He leveled her with a stern look. "She won't be in town for long."

"Good." With her chin high, she kept a firm grip on her backpack.

"I think you two need to clear the air."

"There's no air to clear. She has her life. I have mine. I don't wish her ill, Dad. I'm tired of being hurt."

He sighed. "Have supper with us."

"Tonight?" She may have sounded a touch too horrified.

He nodded.

"I can't." She could, but she didn't want to. Needed time to prepare first. However, Dad wouldn't let up until she agreed.

"How about tomorrow?" he asked.

How about never? She closed her eyes, found her bearings and nodded. "Fine."

"Come over after work." He gave her a hug. She barely returned it.

"Want me to bring anything?"

"Nope. Just yourself."

They said their goodbyes, and she sat in her truck without starting it. She needed someone to talk to. And the only person she wanted to talk to was Cade.

Without giving herself a chance to change her mind, she called him.

"What's up?"

"I know you're with your mom and you have Tulip, but is there any way we could talk?"

"Just a sec." Muffled voices left her no idea what was being said. "I'll swing by your place in a few minutes."

"Okay." Her heart lightened. He ended the call without responding, and she didn't care. Was he bringing his mom and the dog? She, personally, would love to have Tulip there, but she didn't really want Christy to hear their conversation. She simply wanted to talk to Cade alone.

As soon as she got home, she brushed her hair and threw on some clean shorts and a short-sleeved shirt. A knock on the front door kicked up her nerves a notch, and she half jogged to open it.

Cade stood there with Tulip in his arms. Other than that, he was alone. A smile spread across his face. The way he looked at her made her feel feminine. Pretty. Special.

"What's going on?" He brushed past her. Whatever cologne he wore should be outlawed. It smelled that good.

"Thanks for coming over." She peered outside before closing the door. "Where's your mom?"

"I dropped her off at her friend's house, and Ty's going over there to take her home. I thought you might want Tulip here."

"I do." She took the dog from him and hugged her. "You're the best, you know that, girl?"

Her tail wagged swiftly. Mackenzie set her down, and she went straight to the kitchen, where her empty dog dishes still sat on the mat. The dog looked back as if she'd been betrayed. "I'm sorry, Tulip. I'll get you some food and water."

After filling the bowls, Mackenzie joined Cade again. "Are you hungry?"

"I'm always hungry." He'd taken off his cowboy hat and was running his fingers through his hair.

"Pizza?"

"Cowboy John's?"

"Of course." She might have only lived here a month, but it hadn't taken long to figure out Cowboy John's pizza was delicious. She placed the order and directed Cade to the living room, where she got comfortable on the couch as he lowered his frame onto the oversized chair kitty-corner to her. Tulip trotted over and put her little front paws up on the edge of the cushion near Mackenzie.

"You want up?" She lifted the dog and waited while she settled on her lap.

"What's going on?" He gave her his full attention, and she got lost in his concerned blue eyes.

"Dad insists I join him and my mother for supper tomorrow." She absentmindedly stroked Tulip's fur. Tulip, in turn, licked the back of her other hand.

"Are they getting back together or something?"

"Eww." She grimaced. "I hope not. I don't think so. They didn't have the best marriage to begin with. I'm guessing your parents did."

He shrugged. "They loved each other. But they argued, too. Dad was steady, and Mom's...well... Mom."

"I wish I knew what to do. My whole life, I've followed a checklist. Get good grades. Apply to colleges. Gain enough experience to get into the vet program. Graduate. Find a job. Open my own practice. With my career, I know what to do. But with my mother? I don't."

She'd never admitted any of that, not even to herself.

"What do you think you should do?" He leaned forward, resting one forearm on the arm of the chair.

Hard question. The Bible said to forgive. But what did that look like? Was Mackenzie obligated to help her mother every time she showed up? Was she supposed to wave and smile as Mom drove away with Mackenzie's hard-earned cash and another chunk of her heart?

"I don't know," she admitted. "I guess I should lower my expectations. Give her what she wants."

"Why would you do that?"

She shrugged. "The pastor's always talking about forgiveness."

"Forgiveness is one thing. I must have missed the section of the Bible where it says to become a doormat."

She snorted in surprise.

Cade stacked one ankle on his opposite knee and leaned back. "I think you can forgive someone without compromising your values."

"Can you? I don't know. I resent every cent I've given her. I must be a scrooge."

"A scrooge? You? Never." His kind smile wriggled under her skin in the best way.

"How would it work?" She kind of got his point, but she couldn't quite grasp the concept. It was as delicate as a spider web in her mind.

"I don't know. For starters, you could set some rules."

Rules. She was good at those. *Rule number one—don't shut me out of your life until you need something from me.*

"My mom would tell you to pray about it." His eyes twinkled. "That's what she tells me."

"Would you tell me the same?"

"Yeah, I would." He squirmed, clearly uncomfortable with where the conversation was heading. He'd been the one to bring it up, though. "But I'm a hypocrite."

"Why? Don't you pray?"

"I pray about a lot of things." His gaze skewered her, and she wondered why he seemed so intense. "But there are things outside of my control. Things I can't change. You live and you learn."

"Like what?" She wanted to know more. She'd told him

about her awkward relationship with her mother. Cade tended to keep his personal stuff to himself. "You keep a lot inside, don't you?"

He stiffened. "Why do you say that?"

"I don't know." The air conditioner kicked on, filling the room with a buzzing sound. "You haven't shared much with me. I mean, I feel close to you, but…there's a lot I don't know. I'm not sure how to describe it."

"What do you want to know?"

"Who was the last girl you dated?"

"Phoebe Armstrong. A paralegal in Casper."

"Why didn't it last?"

"Distance. And I wasn't that into her."

"Have you ever been in love? A serious relationship?"

"I thought I was." He sat back, tapping his fingers on his thighs. "I dated Gia for almost a year. She worked for an art dealer in New York."

Her heart shriveled as he talked. Gia. The name alone sounded classy. And she'd worked in the art world—in the big city.

The relationship was over, so why did this bother her? *Because you want him for yourself.*

"Why did it end?" She braced herself for him to tell her about his broken heart.

He hesitated before answering. Gia must have hurt him really badly.

"She wanted to move in together. For years, I'd been getting further from God, and when she gave me an ultimatum, it kind of hit me. What was I doing? Who was I? What were my values? I broke up with her. The following week, my dad visited for a few days."

"Did he give you a pep talk?" she said brightly.

"I guess you could say that." His expression grew sad.

"You must miss him a lot, don't you?"

He swallowed, nodding.

A knock on the door startled her. The pizza. Cade stood, holding his palm out. "Stay there. I'll get it."

Soon, the aroma of mozzarella and pepperoni wafted to her. She nudged Tulip off her lap and joined Cade in the kitchen. While he opened the refrigerator for sodas, she pulled plates out of the cupboard. They returned with their hands full to the living room and dug into their slices.

"I've told you about my dating past, so it's only fair you tell me yours." He watched her in between bites. "How many hearts did you break?"

"Me?" She sputtered as her soda went down the wrong tube. She thumped her chest. "None."

"Yeah, right. There had to have been a college romance."

"I mean, I dated here and there." And cut things off quickly with each guy.

"You didn't find the one, huh?"

"Nope." She hadn't given any of the guys much of a chance, either. "I was pretty focused. The minute they got in the way of homework, I ended things."

"Really?" He drew the word out. "They must not have been very exciting."

"I'm not looking for exciting."

"What are you looking for?"

You. Heat climbed her neck. She kept her attention on her half-eaten slice. "I don't have much to offer a man at this point. My time is limited."

"That's not what I asked." His eyes shimmered with something that made her pulse quicken. Dangerous. This conversation was loaded with explosives.

"I don't know, Cade." She shouldn't have said his name. It felt too intimate. "I'm not really looking for anything."

"My mom would say that's when you're most likely to find it. But I don't listen to my mom about stuff like that. She reads too many romance novels."

"What are *you* looking for?"

The shimmer vanished. "I've got all I need."

She couldn't argue with that. He was successful, well liked, had a great family—

"Actually, that's a lie." He set his empty plate on the end table and joined her on the couch. Tulip looked up from the corner cushion where she was napping, then she closed her eyes again.

What was he doing? Her heart began to pound. Mackenzie set her plate on the coffee table.

"I'm not looking for anything, but if I was," Cade shifted to face her and ran the back of his finger down the hair framing her face, "I'd be partial to strawberry blond hair and deep blue eyes."

Her mouth went dry, and all she could do was blink.

"I'd also be way too interested in a mobile vet trailer if she had one, and I wouldn't mind running with her to hide from my mom and her matchmaking buddies during a festival."

Mackenzie didn't know much about flirting, and she didn't have much experience with whatever was happening to her pulse. But one thing she did know was if Cade kissed her, she'd have no objections.

He must have read her mind. His hand slid behind her neck, and he leaned closer. Pressed his lips to hers. And she let out a soft sigh. Then he held her closer, and she wrapped her arms around his neck. His embrace was the support she didn't know she needed. His kiss was the connection she'd been missing.

She'd never realized how alone she'd been all these years. Never knew she could be necessary to someone. But the way his mouth pressed to hers spilled secrets she'd never anticipated. He really liked her. As she kissed him back, she reveled in new sensations, throwing her fears and doubts aside.

When he drew away, his eyes crinkled in the corners, and she could see the little boy he'd been.

"I've wanted to do that for a while."

"Oh, yeah?" Why did she feel so out of breath?

He nodded, taking her hand and raising the back of it to his lips. "Yeah."

He continued to sit next to her as they talked about everything and nothing for the next couple of hours. Finally, he stood and helped her to her feet. He slid his hands around her lower back, staring into her eyes. "Thank you. This was the best night I've had in a long time."

"Same here." She wanted to lean into his strong chest, and so she did. He held her tightly, and she savored his strength and warmth.

"Call me tomorrow after supper with your parents. Let me know how it goes."

Her parents. Right. She stepped back, giving him a weak smile. "I will."

He kissed her again before gathering his hat, picking up Tulip and heading out the front door. He paused on the first porch step and looked back at her. She waved. He hitched his chin toward her and left.

As soon as she shut the door, anxiety and excitement kicked in. She really liked Cade, but she didn't want to be this close to him. To fall in love was too scary. Too unpredictable.

She padded back to the living room.

You're flirting with the danger zone.

Yeah, she was, and she didn't know how to stop it. And she wasn't sure she could if she tried.

Chapter Ten

Cade had been fighting an uneasy feeling all day. He didn't know why, either. Trent's flight had been delayed, but he'd be arriving within the hour for the interview. Licorice seemed to be settling in fine. Ty had dropped off the horse bright and early. They'd put her in a paddock adjacent to the horse pasture. One by one, the horses kept stopping near their shared fence line to check her out. So far, Licorice had been the most taken with Tulip. The dog kept running over to the fence, and Licorice would drop her head to sniff her. It was cute. Best buds already.

Cade would have to mention it to Mackenzie later. She'd be proud to know that Tulip was helping the horse get settled. *Wait.* He smacked his forehead. He couldn't tell her about it. The horse was a surprise. A thank-you gift. Once Tulip passed her Canine Good Citizen test, Cade planned on bringing Mackenzie out to give her Licorice.

Maybe the uneasiness had something to do with last night's unbelievable kiss.

He called Tulip's name, and she instantly left the horse to race to Cade's side. He chuckled. "You're getting good at that. Come on. It's time to get spoiled by Mom."

As they made their way to the house, he studied the ranch. Everything appeared to be in order. Potted flowers brightened the back deck. The house itself showed no signs of wear and tear. He and Tulip entered through the sliding doors off the deck, and he yelled that he was back. Mom stood in the kitchen with Tulip's vest in her hand.

"Just let me grab the treats. I'm working with her on meeting other dogs today. Angie's bringing Duke, and Mary's borrowing her son's beagle. We're going to walk up and down the sidewalks, then treat ourselves to lunch from Dixie B's and a box of candy from R. Mayer Chocolates."

"Sounds good, Ma." He washed his hands as she flitted here and there gathering Tulip's things. If she was this bad fussing over a dog, he could only imagine how she would be with a grandchild.

Grandchild?

That thought froze him into a statue. He hadn't thought much about kids, but after last night's kiss, he could see himself holding a baby girl with blue eyes.

Whoa, there. You're getting ahead of yourself.

No one had said anything about kids or marriage or…love.

He bowed his head. *Lord, I'm flirting with disaster, aren't I?*

"Ready?" Mom held Tulip under one arm, with her leash in hand and humongous purse over her shoulder.

"Yep."

Out in the driveway, he held the truck door open for her and helped her get settled. Then he strapped Tulip in her doggy seat and began the drive to town.

"I think it's great you're hiring Trent." Mom watched the scenery go by. "I always liked him. He and Ty had a lot in common when they were young."

"I haven't decided if I'm hiring him or not. We'll see how the interview goes and if he even wants the job."

"Why wouldn't he want it?" Her indignant tone made him smile. "It's home. Caring for horses."

He wouldn't argue. She was probably right.

An unfamiliar urge kicked in—the urge to ask his mother for advice. About Mackenzie. Would she take it the wrong way? Start bombarding him with truth bombs he didn't want to hear? Did he even know what he wanted to ask? The last thing he needed was for his mother to start mentally planning a wedding. Not that she didn't on a daily basis, anyhow, but still.

"Can I ask you something?" He gave her a sideways glance. Her forehead wrinkled with curiosity.

"Go ahead."

"How did you know you were in love with Dad?" He winced. Why had those words spilled out of his mouth? That wasn't what he wanted to ask.

"I was in love with him long before I was ready to admit it." She stared out the front window with a soft smile on her lips. "Pete was patient. He knew I had a lot going on."

"Like what?"

"Relationships weren't my strong suit. My mother and I never saw eye to eye, and I don't think I had any idea what real love looked like."

He'd never met his maternal grandmother. "What did your mom do?"

"It wasn't so much what she did. It was more that I couldn't live up to her expectations. And she kind of checked out of our family when I was small. She was there physically, and that was about it. I didn't really have a mother, and it affected me."

Sympathy made him want to comfort her, but he kept his hands on the wheel.

"I don't think I really got the strength to consider marrying Pete until Trudy and I spent time together. She was so patient and kind. She'd ask about my day. Your nana was genuinely interested in me, my job and my life."

"Sounds like you fell in love with her," he teased.

"In a way, I did. She helped me see there were better mothers, that I could be one like her. I don't pretend to say I've been as good of a mom as she was, but she's my role model. My friend, too. Your dad could have given up on me—he almost did at one point—but he didn't. I never deserved him, and I'm grateful every day that he was mine. I can't imagine what my life would have been like without him and you boys."

"You deserved him. And you're a great mom. The best." The words were gruff, and he cleared his throat. All these emotions had been sneaking up on him as she spoke. "I take you for granted, and I'm sorry."

When she didn't reply, he flicked her a glance and realized she was stealthily wiping away tears.

Great. He'd made her cry.

"Thank you. I appreciate it." She squeezed his arm. "And you don't take me for granted. You're a good son. You drive me everywhere. Never complain about it. I'm blessed."

He cleared his throat, then steered the conversation to discuss everything Tulip needed to practice before her test, and before long, Cade was dropping Mom and Tulip off on Center Street. He waved to Angie and Mary, then made the short drive to the construction site to meet with Trent. His phone rang as he parked.

"Cade speaking."

"I have a few questions." Michael Grove's deep voice sounded annoyed. "Paris showed me the pictures of your barns and grounds and explained what you were offering."

Finally. The owner of Forestline Adventures must be seriously considering using Moulten Stables if he was calling him personally. Cade got out of the truck and ambled toward his makeshift office as Michael asked about how many horses they could reasonably house over the winter, the type of exercise they'd receive, their security system and liability policy. Cade answered everything with ease.

As Cade entered the office, Michael mentioned the one subject he'd been dreading. "I'm assuming you'll have an equine-certified veterinarian on call."

"I'll have a qualified vet on call." He kept his tone neutral.

"Qualified? That's not what I said."

"I can send you the link to Dr. Howard's website. She has a state-of-the-art mobile vet trailer, and she's within five minutes of the stables."

"If I'm trusting you with my horses, I have to have the best. I'll be paying top dollar, and you know it."

This wasn't about money. Cade understood the game all too well. It was about status, bragging rights, luxury.

"You'll have the best." But was it true?

"I'll think about it."

They ended the call, and Cade pocketed his phone. The veterinarian issue would work itself out. If it didn't, he'd be stuck with an expensive, top-of-the-line barn with no horses to fill it.

Mackenzie couldn't imagine a more awkward meal if she tried. She sliced off a chunk of baked chicken and chewed it slowly so she wouldn't have to contribute to the conversation.

Mom had been overcompensating since the minute Mackenzie arrived, gushing over her outfit—it was a basic navy T-shirt and shorts, nothing special—and how great the clinic was and how she'd love to see her house.

Dad kept giving Mackenzie concerned glances. She wanted to roll her eyes and tell them both to stop it, but she didn't. She'd play along. Eat the chicken and her salad. Pretend everything was fine.

It wasn't fine. It hadn't been fine since she was a little girl.

"Your clinic seems to be doing well." Her mother's eyes pleaded with her—for what, Mackenzie didn't know—as Mom buttered a roll.

"It is." She stabbed a bite of lettuce and cucumber onto her fork.

"Why don't you tell me about it?" Mom asked her.

Mackenzie finished chewing before responding. "I treat mostly dogs and cats. Last week, someone brought in an injured raccoon."

"Oh, that sounds exciting." Mom nodded brightly. "And have you gotten over your fear of horses?"

Irritation gripped her fingers into claws. "I'm not afraid of horses. I've never been afraid of horses."

"Oh, well, I just thought the surgery with the horse that died affected you." With her eyes downcast, her mother fiddled with the napkin in her lap.

"I'm fine." She shoveled a piece of chicken in her mouth before she said something she regretted. What was Dad's point in hosting this meal? What did her parents hope to accomplish?

The sounds of silverware scraping on plates filled the otherwise silent room. Charger lay on his dog bed with his head resting on his crossed front paws.

"He's come a long way." Mackenzie gestured to the dog.

"Yes, we've been spending a lot of time together." Dad gave the German shepherd an affectionate smile. "He's much better behaved than when I first picked him up. Our evening runs have been helping him burn off some of his energy."

"Have you made a decision about what contractor to use for the center?" she asked.

"Ed McCaffrey. I'll have to wait until September for him

to start, but I think it will be worth it. After years of working full-time, I could use a break."

"I'm enjoying my break." Mom's smile didn't reach her eyes. "I'd enjoy it even more if I could catch up with you, Mackenzie. I haven't even seen your house."

She debated how to respond. Last night, Cade had made a good point about rules and not being a doormat. Did her mother even know why Mackenzie felt the way she did? They hadn't discussed it. There hadn't been any opportunity to talk about it. If her mom hadn't ghosted her, maybe.

"I don't feel safe spending time with you, Mom." There, she said it. She set her fork down and hoped her heart wouldn't beat right out of her chest.

"Safe?" Mom let out an incredulous laugh. "What are you talking about? I would never hurt you."

"You do hurt me. Every time we do this—" she waved her hands "—whatever this is. I fool myself into thinking you miss me, and you don't."

"How can you say that? I *do* miss you. I wouldn't have come to Jewel River for any other reason."

"That's not true. You're here because you want something from me. Not because you miss me. Not because you want to spend time with me. I don't know—maybe you actually believe the words you tell me. I don't. Not anymore."

"I see." Mom tucked her chin and blinked rapidly. Was she crying?

"Let's not say things we'll regret." Dad stared at Mackenzie, then glanced at Mom.

"The only thing I regret is not saying these things years ago." She hiked her chin. "I think it's time to get it all out there."

"Careful." Her father leveled a stern look her way. She ignored it.

"Mom, I find it incredibly painful when you show up, include me in your plans to start over with a new job in a new town, then borrow money from me and go silent. I wanted— expected—to hear how your new job was going. I wanted to know if you'd gotten settled into your apartment okay, if you'd made any friends. But you wouldn't respond to my texts beyond saying everything was fine. And within a few weeks, you no longer responded at all."

"I was busy." Her eyes grew round. "I didn't want to bother you."

"Bother me? No. Hearing from you wouldn't bother me. It's what people who are close to each other do. They support each other. I wanted to be emotionally supportive."

"But you are. You're always supportive."

"Only when you allow it. It's always on your terms, Mom." Her throat tightened with emotion. She didn't dare look at her father. Didn't need to see the censure and disappointment sure to be in his eyes. "Every time you arrive, I get my hopes up. I enjoy being with you. I even like helping you get a plan together. Then you take my money and run. It makes me feel used. Rejected."

She wished Tulip was on her lap. She didn't know what to do with her hands, so she clasped them tightly, rubbing her thumbs over each other. Her mother's face was pinched and pale. Dad appeared ready to throw in his two cents on the issue.

And all Mackenzie wanted to do was leave.

"Your mother loves you."

"No offense, Dad, but I don't think you understand the situation." She hadn't told him about all the money she'd given to her mom over the years. Hadn't told him much about their relationship at all.

"Do I understand the situation?" he asked her mother.

"Neither of you has any idea what my life is like." Color bloomed in her mother's cheeks. Her voice grew shrill. "You're both over here making your dreams come true. Opening a service-dog training center—what you always wanted. And you—" she pointed to Mackenzie "—a veterinary clinic. Again, your lifelong dream. I don't have one of those. I'm almost sixty, and I don't know what to do with my life. I can't hold on to jobs for long. I don't even know if I want to anymore."

Mom pushed her chair back to stand.

"No one is leaving this table." Dad had his firm voice on. "We're hashing this out. Right now."

"What do you think is going to happen, Dad?" Mackenzie sighed, tired of the drama. "Why is it so important to you that we all get along?"

"It just is," he mumbled.

"Fine." She pushed her plate away. "Mom, if you'd like to have me in your life, you're going to have to make an effort with me. No more showing up on my doorstep without any warning. You can make plans ahead of time and stay in a hotel. I'd like to hear what you're doing, but I will not be giving you any money to do it. And please don't think we'll be diving into your fantasy of what you think our relationship should look like. We're not going to be besties anytime soon."

Both her mom and her dad stared at her with matching stunned expressions.

Mom licked her lips, pressing them together. "You make it sound like I have some sinister plan. It's not like that."

"Then what is it like? Help me understand."

Her shoulders sank like a balloon deflating. "I start a new job, and I think *This is it. This time I've found it.* Then I give it a go, and it falls apart. I don't know why. It just does. And it's all so tiring. I don't expect you'd understand because you're like your father. Steady. Smart. Committed. And I'm not."

Her mother had never admitted any flaws or vulnerability in the past.

"You have other qualities, Bonnie." Kindness emanated from her father. "You're always too hard on yourself."

Too hard on herself? The woman wasn't hard enough on herself, in Mackenzie's opinion. She got a free pass for all her bad behavior.

Her mother's lower lip wobbled, but she nodded. Then she glanced at Mackenzie. "I do want to be part of your life."

Mackenzie wanted to believe her, but she couldn't. It would take time for Mom to earn her trust.

"What you said is fair," Mom said, sniffing. "We'll try it your way. It's not as if my way ever works."

Sympathy gripped her, and she tried to push it away. This was how it started. She'd feel bad for her mom, take her in, help her get on her feet and…end up getting burned.

One meal together would not solve their problems.

But maybe it was a start.

Chapter Eleven

Cade held his breath the following Tuesday as he and his mother waited for the verdict in the back room of the clinic. Patrick had just finished guiding Mom and Tulip through each step of the Canine Good Citizen test, but he still hadn't looked up from his clipboard. Tulip had excelled at most of the tasks: She'd sat quietly while Patrick came up and greeted Mom. She'd allowed Patrick to pet her. Then he'd checked her ears, teeth and nails before instructing Christy to walk her from cone to cone as he observed that the tension in the leash stayed loose.

Although it was their day off, Emily and Greta had stopped by to help with the test. They'd entered the back room of the clinic and wandered around while Christy walked Tulip. The dog had ignored them as she should.

Afterward, Patrick observed Mom giving Tulip basic commands like sit, down and stay. Cade had gotten a little nervous when Mackenzie brought in Charger, but while Tulip had perked up, she continued to sit near Mom's feet until Patrick had the dogs walk past each other. Later, when Patrick purposely knocked over a bin to see how Tulip would react to a commotion, the dog barely noticed.

The only unknown element at this point was how Tulip had responded to two minutes alone with Patrick. He'd explained that she needed to stay calm with him and not bark or whine while Cade and Christy were out of the room.

"Good news." Patrick looked up from the clipboard with a grin. "She passed with flying colors. Congratulations. Tulip is now a certified Canine Good Citizen."

Mom scooped up the dog. "Did you hear that? You're such a good girl. You passed your test!"

Cade hugged his mom with Tulip between them. Finally. Everything was falling into place. After last week's interview, he'd formally offered Trent Lloyd the position of managing Moulten Stables. Trent would be moving next month into the old house across the road from the property. And Cade was this close to convincing Forestline Adventures to board their horses with him. The cherry on top was Tulip passing her test.

Mackenzie came over to congratulate them, and he gave her a big hug.

"Can we take her to see Nana?" Cade asked her. They'd been spending time together every day. Hugging her and holding her hand had become second nature at this point. He was falling in love with her, and there didn't seem to be any brakes he could press to stop it.

She beamed. "I don't see why not. You've cleared it with the nursing home, and she did well there last week. Just make sure she's wearing her therapy-dog vest."

"I can't believe she passed," Christy said. "We need to celebrate. Why don't you all come out and have supper at our place? We'll grill burgers on the back deck."

"I'm sorry, Christy," Patrick said. "But I told Bonnie I'd help her with something tonight."

"She's welcome to join us."

"That's kind of you, but I have to pass on this one. Excuse me, I'd better get Charger from Greta. Congratulations, again." He strode toward the door.

"What about you, Mackenzie?" Mom had a gleam in her eye, and for once, Cade didn't mind it.

"Sure, why not?"

"Wonderful!" Christy turned to Cade. "We'll have to stop at the supermarket on the way home. We'll get the burgers, buns and some chips and dip."

"Actually, I really want to take Tulip to see Nana first." He'd waited six weeks. He didn't want to wait another minute.

"She'll see her tomorrow, Cade." His mom's expression fell.

Mackenzie gave Cade a thoughtful glance. "Actually, Christy, why don't you ride with me? We'll head to the supermarket while Cade takes Tulip to the nursing home."

"Really?" Mom sounded like she'd won a million dollars. "Okay. I like this plan. It will give us a chance to get to know each other better."

Mom handed him Tulip's leash. "Thanks. I'll see you two in a little while."

Ten minutes later, he and Tulip strolled down the hall of the nursing home to the reception desk.

"Guess who passed her test?" He grinned at Charlene. Her mouth formed an O, and she began to clap. Then she rounded the counter and crouched to pet Tulip.

"You did it, huh? Who's the good girl? You're going to be the queen of this place in no time."

Tulip ate up the attention.

"By the way, I made sure Janey added the *plus one* to your wedding invitation."

"Thanks." He grinned. "We're heading to Nana's."

"Have fun." Charlene gave him and the dog a little wave.

Excitement built as he neared the room. He knocked and entered. The shades were drawn, but the light was on. Nana, in bed, turned her head as he came inside.

"Pete?"

His spirits crashed. "No, Nana, it's me, Cade."

"Come here."

He obeyed.

"I've been thinking about it, and you're being too hard on Cade." She must not have gotten the memo that *he* was Cade. "You raised a fine man, Pete. He knows right from wrong."

A prickly sensation spread over his skin. What was she talking about?

"This business in New York isn't worth getting all worked up over." She clutched his hand tightly.

New York? Had Dad told Nana about their fight that weekend? Had he given her *all* the details? Bile rose in his throat.

"Okay," he said. Should he leave? He didn't think he could handle whatever else she planned on sharing.

"He's a good boy." Nana rested her head against the pillows, patting his hand. "Cade's not doing anything wrong."

That was what she thought. Cade bowed his head and saw Tulip waiting patiently at his feet. Tulip. The whole reason he was here.

His heart wasn't in it anymore. But as he stared at the training vest and the little dog who'd done everything he and his mother had asked, he knew he'd better follow through.

He picked up Tulip and brought her close to Nana's hand.

"I brought the dog I told you about."

"Dolly?" She brightened.

"No, Tulip. The Pomeranian."

"Oh, she's cute." Nana's face lit up as she smiled. She reached for the dog. "Can I pet her?"

"You sure can." He let Tulip sniff her hand a moment.

"She's soft." Nana looked so happy as she petted the dog. "Hi there, doggy."

"Do you want her on your lap?" he asked.

"Yes."

She petted Tulip for several minutes without speaking. The dog seemed to love it.

"Thanks for bringing Dolly out, Pete."

"You're welcome." His heart was wrung, and tears formed behind his eyes. He tried to keep his composure.

"If it makes you feel better, I'm praying for Cade."

"I've got to take off." If she said another word, he'd choke on his emotions. He carefully took the dog in his arms, kissed Nana on the cheek, said goodbye and walked out of the room. He power walked down the hall, waved to Charlene without stopping and headed outside.

Out in the warm sunshine, he sucked in a breath and raised his gaze to the sky.

All this time, he'd thought that no one had known about his falling out with Dad. But he'd been wrong.

Nana had known. Nana knew.

And worse, she'd given him the benefit of the doubt. For years, Nana had thought the best of him, and he didn't deserve it.

The triumphant feeling he'd been anticipating from having Tulip visit her was nowhere to be found. He strode to the truck and strapped Tulip into her doggy seat. As he drove home, all he could think was that he couldn't keep living a lie.

He had to tell Mackenzie the truth about his job in New York City.

And once he did, he'd walk away from her, like he should have done from the beginning.

Cade was being unusually quiet. Mackenzie glanced his way as she stood to gather plates. The burgers had been delicious, and spending time with Christy had given her a new appreciation for the woman. She'd asked Mackenzie thought-

ful questions and had been genuinely interested in her re-
sponses. Cade and Christy were more alike than Mackenzie
realized.

Last week, when Mackenzie had filled him in on the supper with her parents, he'd told her he was impressed that
she'd been honest about her feelings. She was impressed
with herself, too. Usually, all her pain festered inside. Since
then, her mother hadn't reached out to Mackenzie. No surprise there. When had her mother ever played by anyone's
rules but her own?

At least she had Cade to look forward to every evening
when he stopped by. The way he listened, the way he hugged
her, the way he kissed her—he made her feel important.

"Why are you so quiet?" Christy frowned at Cade. The sun
dipped lower in the sky, casting shadows on the back lawn
below the deck.

"Am I?"

Mackenzie exchanged a glance with Christy. *Yes.*

"Must have been all the excitement." His lips tightened
into a not-quite smile. "Mackenzie, would you like to take
a walk?"

"Sure. Let me clear some of these plates first."

"Oh, no." Christy shooed her away. "I'll take care of this.
You two go."

"Ready?" Cade stood and hitched his head toward the
stairs.

"Sure."

Neither spoke until they were halfway down the lane that
led to the outbuildings.

"I take it the visit with your grandmother earlier didn't
go well?" she asked. There was something off about him,
and over the past couple of weeks, she'd gotten to know him
pretty well. Enough to care about him. Deeply.

"Nana loved petting Tulip." The words sounded strangled.

"I'm not surprised." She breathed in the air, heavy with summer, and tried to come up with why he was acting weird. Nope. Nothing.

When they reached the horse stables, they continued down the aisle until they came to a stack of hay bales at the end, where another set of doors were open.

"Mackenzie, I need to tell you something." He gestured for her to sit on the hay bales. A sense of impending disaster filled her body, so she remained standing. He shifted his attention to his cowboy boots. "I haven't been honest with you."

Her muscles locked as her brain started spitting out endless scenarios. Was he seeing someone? Had he been married? Was he still married? Did he have kids she didn't know about?

"I'm not who anyone thinks I am." He stared off through the open doors to the pastures beyond. She didn't say a word. Just stood there with her arms by her side, watching him.

He'd murdered someone. Sold drugs. Buried a body in the woods near his old fort.

"Back when I was in New York, I worked for a global investment bank. I moved up the ranks quickly, and they asked me to join a special team that was working on new financial products for investors. I knew I'd be great at it because of the way my brain is wired. At the time, I was caught up in the Wall Street culture, competing against everyone else to get ahead."

No kids? No dead bodies? What did banking have to do with anything?

"I, and the rest of our team, worked with a few of the best coders in the world, and together we created the products our bosses wanted. I won't—and legally can't, due to nondisclosure agreements—get into the details, but everything we created was basically just a new way to charge fees."

"Fees? What's wrong with that?" She was missing something, wasn't she?

"Almost every time these investments are touched, it generates a fee—if not multiple fees—and they're hidden from the customer."

"Is that illegal?"

"Technically, no. Not the way we were doing it. Fees are supposed to be transparent to clients. But we found loopholes. Although the lawyers and my supervisors assured me everything was legal, I knew it was wrong. We were making the fees virtually untraceable. The company made more money from these products than anyone could have imagined. I was a hero. The entire team was. And in exchange for praise, bonuses and promotions, I ignored my conscience."

Mackenzie frowned as she realized how torn up Cade was about this.

"It all came to a head when my dad visited. I wanted to impress him. Took him to the best restaurants. We ran into people from my company, who told Dad what a great job I was doing. Not long before my father left, he looked around my expensive apartment and asked me what I did, exactly, to earn all my money. I knew that tone, and I got defensive."

She knew all about getting defensive. Every interaction with her mother made her bristle.

He stared off into the distance. "I gave him the sugarcoated version. Then he stared at me hard and said, 'Lie to yourself, but don't lie to me.' It was like he knew how many ethical lines I'd crossed. I don't think I even realized how many I'd crossed until that moment. I got mad. We argued. And I was fuming when he looked me in the eye and said,

'Don't lose sight of what's important in all your wheeling and dealing. It ain't money, son.'"

Her heart hurt for him, disappointing his father like that.

"A few weeks later, I stood next to Mom for his funeral."

"I'm sorry, Cade." She didn't know what else to say. Her muscles tensed as she waited for him to spell out the real problem. Whatever else he was about to confess would likely shock her.

"I am, too." His eyes held something wild as he looked anywhere but at her. "Now you know why I haven't gotten serious with anyone."

Wait. That was it?

"Not really."

"The unethical side of me is still there, still a part of me. I can't get rid of the restlessness that drives me. I'm always looking for loopholes. Constantly searching for my next venture. I tried to be like my dad—content with ranching—and I couldn't do it. Every morning, I'm analyzing stocks and investments. Then I'm on the phone with a real estate agent about upcoming auctions on properties. Next thing I know, I'm stopping in at the construction zone of the stables. My mind comes up with fifteen different businesses to start every single day. I can't turn off this part of me. I can't turn any of it off!"

Mackenzie took a step backward. She would have preferred to step forward, to put her hand on his arm and reassure him. But she didn't. Couldn't.

"Why are you telling me this?" She rubbed her forearms.

"Because you deserve to know."

"Why?"

"You just do."

"There's more to it. Why are you telling *me* this?"

He met her gaze. "I'm not good enough for you. You think

I'm a decent guy, but I'm not. The real me is a mess. I'm sorry. I'm sorry I wasn't honest with you."

And there it was. The real reason for his confession. To drive her away. To end their relationship. Tears sprang up, and she struggled with her emotions.

In this moment, she could finally acknowledge the truth. She'd fallen in love with him. And it wasn't enough. Her love would never be enough for him.

She'd had enough experience with her mother to understand that. Either Cade would push her away because deep down he didn't care about her, or if she did matter to him, he'd convince himself pushing her away was the noble thing to do.

She let out a heavy sigh. Now what?

Should she leave? Accept the fact he'd made up his mind?

No, she wouldn't let him push her away without fighting for him.

"Don't I get a say in this?" Her palms grew moist.

"You don't understand." He strode out of the stables to the nearby fence, where horses were grazing. Mackenzie joined him there.

"Cade." She touched his arm.

"Do you see that beautiful Morgan horse grazing? It's the small black one." He pointed to where two horses flicked their tails. "I bought her for you. To keep at my stables so you can come over and ride her whenever you want. Don't worry about taking care of her. My crew will do that."

"What?" Too stunned to respond, she tried to process what he was saying. "I don't want a pony from you, Cade. I'm not a five-year-old girl."

"It's not a pony. It's a—"

"I know what it is. It's a guilt offering. And a poor substitute for what I really want."

"What do you really want?" His eyes glistened with pain. Regrets mounted in them.

"I want you. I care about you. Your past is what it is. Do you think I'm perfect?"

"Yeah, I do."

"I'm not. I caused the death of a pregnant mare *and* her foal during my residency. The family sued me. For the record, I was acquitted." She couldn't believe she was telling him this without getting emotional. "I kept it from you." She shrugged. "Now you know I have things in my past I'm not proud of, either."

"I'm sure you did the best you could. It wasn't your fault."

"And I'm sure you were young and ambitious and wanted to please your supervisors."

"It's not the same."

"I know it isn't. But you recognized you weren't living the way you should, and you changed."

"Only because my dad died."

"You would have quit your job even if your dad had lived. You'd already been making changes. You broke up with Gia, right?"

"See?" He pushed his hands off the fence and shifted to face her. "You think I'm someone I'm not. I wouldn't have quit. I liked being a big shot."

"You would have," she said quietly. "God got through to you."

"By punishing me! My dad's gone."

"Like that's your fault? *You* caused him to get cancer?"

"No, but—"

"What exactly are you beating yourself up over? What do you have to prove? And who are you trying to prove it to?"

"I'm just being honest. Showing you the real me. The way I should have done from day one."

"Fine." She threw her hands up. "You're a terrible person. Is that what you want to hear? I've been around you. I know you're restless. I know you need your hands stoking eight different fires. None of it matters to me. I don't want some perfect guy. I want you, not Mr. Wonderful!"

All the energy drained from him, and his eyes were sad as he shook his head. "You don't get it."

"I get it. You're the one who doesn't get it. I see more than you know. And you see more about me than most people do. Do you care that I have no hobbies? No. And I'm sure it hasn't escaped your notice, I'm a loner. I get panicky any-time someone wants me to join a group, and I've basically cut my mother out of my life. I'm not perfect, Cade, and you accept me anyhow."

He opened his mouth, but she held her hand up.

"Keep your horse," she said and tightened her jaw. "You know where to find me if you can get it through your dumb head that I'm not interested in perfect. I just want someone who isn't afraid to be real."

It was her turn to pivot. She marched all the way to her truck, started it up and drove away.

She wasn't going to sit around waiting for him to figure out she was worth fighting for. She'd done that for years with her mother. She was going home and getting on with her life. Alone.

Chapter Twelve

That had been a disaster. Cade waited until Mackenzie's truck faded from view, then he marched to the house.

"Where's Mackenzie?" his mom asked. He didn't answer. He went straight to his bedroom and shut the door.

Soft footfalls warned him his mother was incoming. *Knock, knock.*

He wanted to yell, "Go away!" the way he'd done countless times as a kid, but he was all grown up now, and his mom didn't deserve that.

"What happened?" Mom asked on the other side of the door. "Can I crack the door open for Tulip to go in there?"

"Yeah." The door opened, and Tulip raced inside. He picked her up and set her next to him on the bed. She scrambled onto his lap, licking his hand. Mom didn't close the door, just watched him from the doorway with a worried expression.

"Cade…"

Grr… He might as well get it all off his chest with his mother, too. Seemed he was in a confessional mood. "Just come in."

She glided through the doorway and sat on the edge of the bed next to him.

"Mackenzie left, and she's not coming back."

"Ever?"

He shrugged. "I don't know. It's not likely."

"What did you say to her? Why did she leave?"

"I told her the truth about me." He turned to face her, and the questions crossing her face brought an emptiness to his stomach. He should have told her this years ago. Would have saved him the pain of carrying around all this guilt. "Dad knew my job in New York wasn't anything to be proud of. He saw the truth within five seconds of arriving in the city."

"New York?" Worry lines tightened around her lips. "What does your father have to do with Mackenzie?"

"Everything." He kept a hand on Tulip and shook his head. "Nothing. I don't know anymore. Everyone around here—including you—thinks I had this great job in New York and that I gave up a lucrative spot on Wall Street to manage the ranch here, but they don't know the truth."

He proceeded to tell her everything he'd told Mackenzie. When he finished, he hung his head and waited for her to lecture him on how disappointed in him she was.

"What do you want me to say?" she asked. "You're a grown man. You made mistakes. You learned from them."

That was it?

Her response wasn't good enough. He deserved a tongue-lashing.

"I didn't learn from them, Ma. I covered them up. Let everyone around here think I'm someone I'm not."

"Oh, please." She gave him a skeptical look and waved as if he was being silly. There was nothing silly about this. "Someone you're not? We're all smarter than that, Cade. We know who you are. Don't think you're such a master at manipulation you could fool an entire town into thinking you're anyone other than who you really are."

He opened his mouth to argue, but she beat him to it.

"After your dad returned from visiting you that weekend, he told me and Nana his concerns. He worried you were on a path that would lead you away from your faith and your values. The three of us prayed for you. And a few days later, Pete went to the doctor, and…well…your city job became the least of our worries."

"But you never said anything." She'd known? All this time? Here he'd thought he'd been keeping this big secret.

"There was nothing to say." Her eyes were bright with kindness. "You moved home, and I could see you doing the right thing. You handled the ranch the way your dad always did. Then you hired Micky. I knew I didn't need to fret. Our prayers for you had been answered. The only thing I worried about was you finding someone to share your life with."

"I didn't see marriage in my future."

"Even now? After meeting Mackenzie?"

His heart finally crashed. He'd pushed her away. She'd been right to be angry about the horse. What had he been thinking giving it to her tonight? After his stupid speech? Had it been to ease his guilt over telling her the truth?

Mom rose. "She's good for you, Cade. Don't let her get away."

Cade stopped breathing as her words registered. *Don't let her get away. She's good for you.* It was practically the same thing Nana had said when she'd thought he was his father.

"And don't try to live up to an unrealistic idea of your dad, either. That man was wonderful, but he was far from perfect." She made it to the door before turning back to him. "Open your Bible and pray. God knows what you need."

It wouldn't do any good. He was too messed up.

The damage had been done, and he didn't know how to fix it.

What an obstinate, irritating, stubborn man. Why had she fallen in love with him?

Nothing could be simple—no, it always had to be hard with her. She hadn't even wanted to fall in love.

Mackenzie pulled into her driveway and groaned at the sight of her mom's old forest green minivan parked on the street.

What was her mother doing on her porch? Like she needed this on top of everything else.

She parked, got out and slammed the door as hard as she could. Stomped like a child all the way to her mom. "What are you doing here?"

"I came to say goodbye." Mom wasn't wearing her fake-happy smile for once. Her demeanor was surprisingly subdued.

"Where are you going?" Mackenzie expected to be pleased at the announcement, but sorrow and regrets weighed on her chest.

"Does it matter?"

She selected her words carefully before responding. Yesterday, it probably wouldn't have mattered. But today, it did. "Yeah, Mom, it does. Want to come inside?"

"Sure."

After unlocking the door, she held it open for her mother. "Nice place."

"Thanks." She closed the door. "Want a quick tour?"

"I'd like that."

Mackenzie showed her around, tucking away each compliment, and steered her to the living room. "Have a seat. Can I get you something to drink?"

"No, I'm fine." She found a spot on the couch. "I want you to know I've been thinking about what you said at supper last week."

Anxiety kicked in. She wasn't sure she wanted to hear her mother's thoughts on her outburst.

Mom fiddled with the hem of her shirt. "I never really put two and two together on how you felt whenever I would leave. Hearing you spell it out was painful. I've been trying to justify my actions—I've had pretend conversations with you for days. It sounds crazy, I know."

Mackenzie knew all about pretend conversations. She had them often.

"But over the past couple of days, it kind of hit me." Mom lifted one shoulder in a sad shrug. "You're right."

She was right? Her mother had never said those words before.

"You're so much like your father." A whisper of a smile lifted her lips. "You're both kind, compassionate. You sacrifice to make other people's lives better. And I'm not like that."

"What are you talking about?"

She gave her head a slight shake. "I don't expect you to understand, Mackenzie. I guess, in some ways, you and your father have always been my last resort."

Ouch. The bottom dropped out of her heart. Of all the cruel things to say.

"And it's because I didn't want to have to rely on you. You've both got your lives together. I doubt you'll ever know what it's like to be down to your last dollar. I make lousy decisions. Can't keep a job for more than a year. Can't save fifty dollars without spending it a week later."

Mackenzie wanted to say something to make her mom feel better, but she didn't have the words.

"Every time I borrowed money from you, I'd leave with the best intentions. I'd tell myself this time was different. That I'd pay you back quickly, and we'd stay in touch, and you'd be proud of me. And a couple of months later, I'd be stressed out, barely keeping it together. I'd want to call you, but I wouldn't. It was too demoralizing to have you know I'd made another mistake. Couldn't be the failure you and I both knew I was."

"You're not a failure, Mom," she said quietly. Compassion stole over her. "I wish you would have called and texted. I could have given you a pep talk. We could have laughed and cried together. I needed you, too."

"Why would you need me? I have nothing to offer." Her eyes filled with tears, and it took everything in Mackenzie to stay seated and not to go hug her.

"I needed *you*, not anything you have." She was getting emotional, and she hated crying. She turned her head away until she could continue. "Do you know how much I used to love when you showed up at my apartment? I loved hanging out with you. Making a game plan for your next job. I loved all of it. But then you'd leave, and you wouldn't talk to me…that was hard, Mom. I had to build a shell over my heart where you were concerned."

"I'm sorry, Mackenzie. I've made a mess of everything. I can't change what I did."

"No, you can't, but maybe we can do things differently from now on."

The hope in her eyes was almost unbearable. Was Mackenzie right to be doing this? Or would she get burned again?

If there was anything Cade had taught her, it was to be honest and to hope for the best instead of keeping everything inside and expecting the worst.

Ironic, considering he'd destroyed her heart tonight.

"Mom, I meant what I said at Dad's. I'm not lending you any more money."

She nodded. "I understand. It's for the best."

"And I need some warning when you're coming to town for a visit."

"I can do that."

"But if you're not going to communicate with me, it doesn't matter. I don't want to be your last resort."

"You're still willing to give me a chance?" Mom asked.

"Yeah. I am. But with rules in place."

"I have a rule, too." She rose, holding out her hands. Mackenzie held her breath. What rule? "Never change who you are. I'm so proud of you, I could cry. You've made something for yourself with your clinic. You're living your dream."

"Thank you, Mom." She did something she couldn't have imagined a day ago. She wrapped her arms around Bonnie Howard and gave her a long, heartfelt hug. "Want to fill me in on your plans?"

"I'd love to. But first, can I take you up on the offer of something to drink?"

"Sure." They went to the kitchen, where Mackenzie took out two sodas and handed one to her mother.

"I found a night job for a hotel in Casper. I think it will be a good fit."

"Where are you going to stay?" The familiar worries rose up about if her mom could handle the job, but as she looked at her mother, she realized she needed to be part of the solution instead of the problem.

Her mother was a grown woman, capable of making it on her own. Mackenzie didn't need to worry about her.

"I'm not sure, yet. I'll find a cheap place until the right apartment comes along."

They talked for half an hour before her mother rose to leave.

"You're going to be fine." She smiled at her mom.

"I know I will. And you will be, too."

They hugged goodbye, and her mother left.

Mackenzie wanted to call Cade to tell him about this unexpected conversation with her mother, but she couldn't. She wouldn't.

She'd spent too much of her life wanting to be important

to her mom. She wasn't wasting a single minute doing the same with Cade. Either he needed her too much to let her go, or whatever they had was over.

And something told her, it was over.

Chapter Thirteen

The following morning, Cade slumped in a chair with Tulip on his lap in his office at the construction site. He'd already met with Micky for their daily ranch meeting. One of Mom's friends had picked her up this morning for some activity they'd planned weeks ago, and he couldn't be more relieved. The last thing he needed was another pep talk/lecture from her.

All he could think about was last night. Mackenzie's pretty face. The words she'd said. *I'm not interested in perfect. I just want someone who isn't afraid to be real.* He alternated between soaring hope and the depressing reality that he wasn't worthy of her love.

He'd prayed last night. Opened the Bible the way Mom had instructed. And he'd been drawn to Isaiah 30:18. The passage basically said the Lord, a God of judgment, will wait in order to give you grace and have mercy on you in order that He may be exalted.

The passage had dropped him to his knees in repentance. Cade deserved punishment, not grace or mercy. He'd asked the Lord for forgiveness for helping the bank he'd worked for cheat people out of their hard-earned money. He'd repented for the words he'd said to his father and for all the ways he'd failed in the years since. Most of all, he asked for forgiveness for trying to hide it all. Hours later, he'd fallen into an uneasy sleep.

"I've been trying to earn it, haven't I, Tulip?" Cade petted the dog. She lifted her head and, panting, smiled at him. Sounds of nail guns and the whir of an air compressor didn't seem to bother her. "I've been going to church my entire life. I've heard the gospel again and again. How could I have missed it so completely?"

The Lord, in His great mercy, had saved Cade from his sins. There was no earning forgiveness. It was free. By grace alone.

His cell phone rang, and he swiped it off the desk and answered.

"Haven't heard from you in a week." Michael Grove sounded annoyed. "Have you addressed Paris's concerns? And where are you at with the veterinarian?"

"What concerns are we talking about?" Usually, he'd be excited to get this call. It meant he was one step closer to sealing the deal. But today, he couldn't bring himself to care about landing Forestline Adventures for the stables.

"The barn. Access. Any bum off the street being around our horses."

Cade kept his temper in check. He'd dropped any thought of dividing the barn after the Fourth of July. Didn't see the point in it. "They aren't bums. They're locals."

"Locals." His tone hit Cade the wrong way.

"Yes. Mostly teenagers on the rodeo team. This is a small town. We all know each other. Besides, I recently hired Trent Lloyd to manage the stables. He has a degree in equine science from Auburn University and has been working for the past ten years at a Thoroughbred farm near Lexington, Kentucky."

"And what does that have to do with access?"

"He grew up in Jewel River. He'll know if someone shouldn't be there."

"How? He's been across the country for years."

Cade tightened his jaw, wanting to chuck the phone across the room. "The people he doesn't know, he'll meet quickly."

"I see." The sound of papers shuffling in the background had Cade raising his gaze to the ceiling. His frustration mounted to dangerous levels. Tulip licked the back of his hand, and his stress immediately lessened. He mindlessly stroked her fur.

The dog was right. There was no reason to get worked up over a call. In fact, there was no reason to get worked up about the stables at all. If Michael didn't want to board his horses, Cade would find someone else. And if no one else wanted his facilities, he had enough money to keep it going for a long time without any outside help.

"What's going on with the veterinarian situation?" Michael asked.

"It's handled. I told you that Mackenzie Howard opened her practice over a month ago. She has her license to treat large and small animals. Her mobile vet trailer is impressive. She can handle any emergency within minutes."

"But she's not certified in equine care."

"No, she isn't. I trust her with my horses, though. She's honest. Her heart is one hundred percent focused on whatever animal she's treating. Your horses couldn't be in better hands."

He meant every word. And he wondered why he'd ever thought her credentials wouldn't be enough.

You were still caught up in that world.

Yeah, he had been. Was he still?

No. He wasn't. Last night, God had finally gotten through to him.

He had absolutely nothing to prove. To anyone. Including Michael Grove.

"I checked the link you sent me and did some research." The man's blustery tone didn't affect Cade one way or the other. "Are you aware she lost a mare and foal and was sued by the owners?"

"Yes, I'm aware." Usually, this would be the point in the conversation where his mind would scramble to offer the man an alternative. But there was no reason to. "She was acquitted. It happened during her residency. I stand by what I said. There's no one I'd trust more with my horses than her."

"Hmm." Michael switched topics and asked about the outdoor arena. A few minutes later, they ended the call.

Cade held Tulip under one arm as he stood. "You and I are going to find Mackenzie. Right now. Because I was dumb, Tulip. I was so stupid. I can't live without her. She's the best thing that's ever happened to me. I can't believe she didn't slap me upside my head last night." Tulip wiggled in his arms as she wagged her tail.

Where should he start? Wednesday—she'd be at the clinic.

"Let's go. Maybe your cuteness will help soften her up. I can't live without her. And I don't care if I have to beg, I'm going to win her back."

Tulip let out a yip and panted up at him.

"That's the spirit."

If she had a job where she could call in sick, she would have stayed home today.

Mackenzie had barely slept last night. Every time she told herself it was over between her and Cade, she'd second-guess herself. Should she fight for him? Try to convince him he wasn't a lost cause?

Why? So he could reject her again? No thanks.

Felt too much like texting and calling her mom only to be ignored.

She checked the GPS again to make sure she didn't miss her turn. Marvin Blythe from Triple B Ranch had talked to Greta this morning about doing wellness checks on all his dogs. Since two of her morning appointments had cancelled, Mackenzie had taken the phone from Greta and told him she'd come out now. Even with the drive, she'd be back in time for her afternoon appointments.

Unfortunately, all this driving was giving her time to think.

And she didn't want to think.

All her thoughts magnetized to Cade. He was the first guy she'd opened her heart to, and he was the only one she could picture having a future with.

Even her old excuse about not having time for a relationship no longer held up. He understood and supported her work. Didn't expect her to be available every minute. They'd found pockets of time to be together last week. Time wasn't the problem.

If he'd just get over his past…

Yeah, like she'd done?

Maybe. After talking with her mother last night, Mackenzie really did think it would be different from now on. She understood the woman better. She'd never realized her mom felt inferior to her and Dad. Her silence made more sense. It didn't excuse her behavior, but at least she'd acknowledged she'd been wrong. And the ground rules they'd set moving forward gave Mackenzie hope that they'd be able to have a relationship of some sort.

What she really wanted was a relationship with Cade.

But not if he wouldn't fight for her.

Pressing the accelerator, she sighed.

She was exhausted, and it wasn't just physical. She was

tired of doubting herself. Tired of being alone. Tired of feeling unimportant.

Finally, the driveway with a big sign overhead spelling out Triple B Ranch appeared, and she turned onto it.

Mackenzie didn't get a chance to park. Marvin ran toward her, waving wildly. She rolled down her window.

"Good, you made it." His jeans, plaid button-down shirt and cowboy boots were dusty and smeared with dirt. His face pinched with concern. "See that driveway? Stop at the third barn. I've got a cow with bloat."

Mackenzie's heart started racing. A bad case of bloat could kill a cow in as little as fifteen minutes. "On my way."

She drove past the barns and parked. Her mind raced with questions. If the bloat wasn't bad, an anti-gas foam might do the trick. But if it was bad? She'd assisted Dr. Johan, but this would be her first time treating it on her own.

She wished Cade was here. He'd boost her confidence and ease her fears because that was what he did. He was that kind of man. One she could rely on.

But he wasn't here. And all she could think of was the horse she'd lost. All that blood. The dead foal slipping out. The owner's ashen face. The kids racing across the lawn, when they should have been kept inside.

All the crying. All the blood.

All her fault.

God, I need You. I'm scared. I can't lose this cow. Don't let me lose this animal. Not this time.

With shaking fingers, she climbed out of the truck and unlocked the trailer. Then she zipped her coveralls over her outfit. Grabbed her supplies and hurried to the barn. Marv was waiting for her in the bay.

"Where is she?" Mackenzie matched his pace as he led her through the barn to the outside corral where he'd put the cow.

"Over there." He pointed, not missing a stride.

"Looks like I got here at the right time." The black cow was almost as wide as she was tall. A bad case of bloat. Just as she'd feared. "Poor girl."

"I'll get her into the chute."

Marv expertly moved the cow into the chute, and Mackenzie checked the animal for signs of other illnesses. No snot or mucus. She listened to its lungs. They sounded clear. The cow's slightly elevated temperature didn't concern her.

Once she'd made it through the examination, her anxiety dissipated, replaced with confidence. She knew how to handle this.

"She doesn't seem to be suffering from an illness like pneumonia. She's got a pretty severe case of bloat, though. I need to get the air out. Are you familiar with a trocar?"

"Yes, ma'am. I've had several cows need them over the years."

"It's our best option at the moment. With your permission, I'll insert one now."

"You've got my permission."

With the supplies ready, she mentally reviewed what Dr. Johan had taught her. She'd watched him insert one only a few months ago. She took out the long, hollow needle and the tool to insert it. After making a small incision in the cow's hide, she poked it through the muscle and rumen wall and began screwing it into place. Marv used his body to keep the cow's haunches steady. The man was an old pro at dealing with sick cattle.

The pitiful moo from the animal tugged at her heart. "I know, sweetheart. Doesn't feel good getting poked. I promise you, though, this will make you feel a whole lot better than you do now."

The sound of gas escaping was music to her and Marv's ears.

"Boy, the air is coming out fast, isn't it?" Marv rounded the chute as Mackenzie went to the front to pet the cow's head.

"She should be feeling a lot of relief. I'll come back in a week or so to take out the trocar."

"I've taken them out before." He patted the cow's side, and then he let her out of the chute. She ran off to the other side of the corral.

"I'd feel better if I came out to have a look at her myself."

Marv gave her a firm nod, took off his hat and wiped his brow with a handkerchief. "I'm mighty obliged. She probably gorged herself in the new pasture. Good growth in there this year."

"Wouldn't surprise me." Mackenzie looked around. "Now, what do you say we take care of your dogs?"

They stopped at her truck so she could take off her coveralls. "I'll drive the trailer up to your garage. It will make it easier. Hop inside."

By the time they reached the house, where the dogs were waiting, she knew how many head of cattle Marv was raising, how he rotated pastures, the supplemental feed he gave the herd in the winter and more.

She got out and followed him through the open garage into the house. Three miniature dachshunds raced to him as soon as he opened the door. The other dogs, minus the Chihuahua, followed with their tales wagging.

"See what I mean?" Jim chuckled, pointing to the Chihuahua his wife held to her chest. "The rat does not like me."

"Gigi is not a rat." The woman shook her head and stepped forward to introduce herself. "I'm Pat, by the way. I'm assuming the cow's okay?"

"She sure is." Marv beamed. "Mackenzie inserted a trocar like an old pro. I'm glad you worked us into your schedule today, or I would have lost that cow."

"God's timing couldn't have been better." She bent to let the dogs sniff her hands. They were all cute. The bassett hounds had plopped on the floor.

"I've lost three cows to bloat over the years. Nothing worse than watching their lungs get compressed to the point they can't breathe." He picked up one of the wiener dogs and cuddled it close. Even dogs who weren't trained as therapy dogs helped make people feel better. Pets were such a blessing.

For the next forty-five minutes, she checked each dog in her trailer. When she was finished, both Marv and Pat acted like she was part of the family. Pat even sent half of a chocolate Bundt cake home with her, and she didn't try very hard to dissuade the woman.

As she climbed into her truck to leave, the couple waved, calling, "Come back anytime."

Before starting the truck, she took a moment to savor what had just happened. She'd known how to handle the emergency. God had given her the experience and the knowledge to save the cow's life.

There was no better feeling in the world.

And if she could handle saving a cow with bloat, maybe she could handle trying to talk some sense into Cade. God had brought them together for a reason. She wasn't going to give him up without a fight.

Chapter Fourteen

❧

"She'll be back this afternoon."

"What time?" Cade held Tulip's leash at the front desk of the clinic.

Greta gave him an apologetic shrug. "I'm not sure. Her next appointment is at half past two, so before then."

Stupid Marv. Having her drive all the way out there for his hundred dogs. Cade wanted to kick the base of the counter, but instead, he gave Greta a tight smile. "I'll stop in later. Would you let me know if she gets back early?"

"Of course, I will. Knowing you're around will put her in a better mood. Those dark circles under her eyes concerned me this morning. Like purple crescent moons, you know? I didn't say a thing because, really, how do you tell your boss she looks haggard? But—"

"I've got to go." He didn't wait for Greta to finish her thought, just urged Tulip to hurry through the waiting room to the door.

Outside, he blew out a frustrated breath. Now what? He couldn't beg Mackenzie for a second chance if she wasn't here.

He wasn't driving all the way back to the ranch.

He was tired of lurking around the unfinished stables.

Ty would be riding around his ranch this time of day, so there was no point heading there.

Cade stared at Tulip. "How about we try Nana again?"

Ten minutes later, he strolled into the nursing home with Tulip in her therapy-dog vest.

"Why, Cade, I didn't expect to see you today." Charlene beamed. "You've got twenty minutes before we bring her down to the cafeteria."

"Thanks. How is she doing?" It didn't really matter how she was. He wanted to sit by her side and hold her hand even if she was sleeping. He'd listen to anything she had to say even if she mistakenly thought he was his father.

He loved her, and he wanted to spend as much time with her while he still could.

"Trudy is having a good day." She nodded brightly. "Go on. See for yourself." Then she bent, talking to Tulip. "And how is our sweetheart doing? Look at you with your spiffy vest. When you're done in there, you come back here for a special treat from your aunt Charlene."

If he wasn't so keyed up, he would have enjoyed the encounter. But his nerves were sizzling hotter than bacon in a cast-iron skillet. He headed down the hall. Pulled back his shoulders. Knocked on Nana's door and entered.

"Cade!" Nana beamed from where she sat in her wheel-chair. "Where's Ty?"

"He's working cattle." He bent to pick up Tulip. "I brought you a surprise."

She covered her mouth with her hands as tears filled her eyes. "A puppy!"

"This is Tulip, the dog we told you about. I brought her over yesterday, but I don't know if you remember."

"You did? I must have been sleeping." She held out both arms, and he set Tulip on her lap. With her tongue lolling, the dog stared at Nana. She gently stroked her fur, exclaiming how soft she was. Tulip did exactly what she was supposed to do—sat calmly and enjoyed the experience.

"Tulip passed her test yesterday. She's all clear to come visit you." He sat in the chair next to her. "We've been training her for over a month. She did really well."

"She's such a dear little puppy." Nana scratched behind Tulip's ears. "And so calm."

"Like Dolly?" he asked.

"Dolly." She jerked her attention to him. "Oh, that's a sweet memory. She was my baby before I had your father. She lived five more years after we brought Pete home."

"What kind of dog was she?"

"I don't know. A mutt. I loved her so." Nana's hand rhythmically petted Tulip. "Thank you for bringing this doggy to visit. Will you bring her again?"

"I will. I can bring her every time I come here if you'd like."

"Yes, I'd love that."

"Nana?"

"Hmm?"

"I think I'm in love."

Her eyes danced with happiness. "What do you mean you think you're in love? Don't you know?"

He cracked his knuckles. "I know. I'm in love."

"Then what's the matter?"

"I've done some things I'm not proud of, and I think she could do better than me."

Nana gave him an understanding smile. "I've done things I'm not proud of, too. We all have. I'm sure your girl has, too. Why don't you let her decide?"

"I told her about it."

"And she broke it off with you?"

"No, I thought it would be best if we went our separate ways, but I was wrong."

"You're scared." Her tender smile was making him squirm. "It's okay. Love is scary."

Tulip let out a contented sigh and closed her eyes.

"I'm going to let you in on a little secret." She wiggled her finger for him to lean in. He did. "Your daddy was terrified of declaring his feelings to your mother."

Dad? Never. The man had always been as calm and collected as could be.

She chuckled. "I finally had to have a talk with him. I was afraid he'd let her get away." She sat back, affectionately petting Tulip. "You Moulten boys can handle just about anything. But love? Whoo-ee. That's scary for you. But when you do give your heart to the right girl, well, you give it all to her. I should know. Your grandpa was the same with me."

His fears vanished. "So you're saying this is a genetic thing?"

"I don't know about that, but it does run in the family."

His chest lightened. A knock on the door made them both turn to see who it was. One of the nurse's aides stood there. "It's time to head to the cafeteria for lunch, Trudy. Oh, I see you have visitors. What a delightful little dog."

"Her name is Tulip," Nana said. "My grandson brought her to visit. Aren't I blessed?"

"You sure are."

Cade stood and plucked Tulip off Nana's lap. Then he set the dog on the floor and held her leash. He kissed Nana's cheek. "I'll be back in a few days. Mom will bring Tulip over tomorrow. I love you."

"I love you, too." She waved. "Don't let your girl get away."

"I won't."

On the way out, he stopped to let Charlene give Tulip a treat and to hear the latest on Janey's wedding plans. Then he drove to Reagan's store and bought every milk-chocolate-covered pretzel she had in stock. With a tender smile, Reagan wrapped pink ribbon around the box and told him he'd made a good choice. She'd thrown in a fresh batch of chocolate-covered strawberries, too.

Next on his list? The supermarket. He bought out the flower department, which wasn't saying much, but still. The only ones he'd left in the store were the potted flowers.

With the backseat of his truck full of bouquets, he drove to the veterinary clinic and sat in his truck to wait until Mackenzie got back.

Nana was right. The Moulten boys might be scared of love, but when they gave their hearts to the right girls, they gave them their all.

His heart was Mackenzie's. And he wanted her to have it, whether he deserved her or not.

Mackenzie's elation over saving the cow fizzled as she neared Jewel River. Yawns kept creeping up on her, and she could barely keep her eyes open. What she needed was a nap. And the rest of the afternoon off so she could figure out what to do about Cade.

She was going to fight for him—no question about it—but she needed a strategy. She needed one soon because she couldn't take sitting with this uncertainty over their future for long.

Closure. She wanted closure.

But she wanted the *right* closure. Not the one where he doubled down on dumb and acted like he was saving her from a fate worse than death by cutting himself out of her life.

The parking lot to the clinic was up ahead. She pulled into it and parked. Only when she got out of the truck did she realize Cade was there. In fact, he was walking toward her with Tulip trotting by his side and his arms full of…flowers?

Hope rose so sharply, it stole her breath.

"Come on, let's go inside." He hitched his chin toward the entrance. She scrambled forward, unlocking and opening the clinic's door—they locked it for lunch—then waited for him and Tulip to go inside before following him in.

Greta and Emily must have gone out to eat because the place was empty. He strode straight to her office and dumped everything onto her desk.

"Do you have a bed here for Tulip?" he asked.

"I do." She opened the closet, took it out and set it on the floor.

"Come," he said to Tulip. She hopped onto the bed, and he had her lie down. She did and promptly fell asleep.

"I've been an idiot." Cade turned to Mackenzie with a gleam in his eyes. "I should have listened to you last night. For years, I've convinced myself I was a terrible person."

"You're not."

"I am," he said, shrugging. "But I'm also saved. Forgiven. And I'm thankful for second chances."

She didn't know what to do with her hands or what to say. He closed the gap between them and took her hands in his. That was better. A sense of calm covered her.

"I want you to know I did not buy the horse for you as some kind of guilt offering. I bought Licorice because I knew you'd love her. I wanted you to have a horse of your own that you could ride at any time. And I knew you didn't want to buy one because you don't have a schedule that would allow you to take care of it. So I will take care of her—well, my staff will. That's all. No strings attached. No guilt involved."

"I believe you." She stared into his eyes and pushed all her doubts and fears aside. Whatever he was going to say next? She was open to it. She couldn't spend another minute doubting his intentions. She'd done it for all those years with her mom, but Cade was different.

"Good, because it's true." He took a breath. "I love you, Mackenzie. I knew you were special the minute I saw you the night Mom and I arrived to meet Tulip."

He thought she was special?

"You're brilliant. Blunt. Beautiful. You're better than me, and I hope you won't let that stop you from giving me a chance." He let go of one of her hands to cup her cheek. "I couldn't even make it twenty-four hours without you. This morning when I woke up, it took everything inside me not to pick up the phone and call you."

She swallowed as joy brought tears to her eyes.

"I know you said you don't have time for a relationship, but I'm flexible. I also know your job is important. It's important to me, too, knowing how much the ranchers and pet owners around here need your expertise. So maybe you could find a way to fit me into your life."

With watery eyes, she nodded, smiling. "I'll fit you in."

"You will?" His eyes shimmered with love, appreciation and maybe even awe.

"I will. I love you, too. I think you're amazing. I think God made you restless for a reason. You help so many people."

"Not really."

She edged closer to him and looked up into his eyes. "You do. You knew this town needed a vet, and you convinced me to move here. You sold the buildings to me and Dad at a steep discount. You trained a therapy dog to make your grandmother happy."

"It was Mom's idea."

"So? You did it with her. You head a committee for a club that exists solely to improve Jewel River. And soon you'll be offering horse boarding at a discount to the community because you want life to be better for them."

"I'm still trying to make a profit on Moulten Stables."

"It's okay to make a profit. And I almost forgot to mention your mother. You drive her everywhere. To keep her safe."

"Trust me. Everyone's safer when she's off the road."

Mackenzie couldn't help but grin. "I love you, Cade. I haven't dated anyone in a long, long time, so forgive me if I'm rusty. I wasn't all that good at it to begin with."

"It's not something you're good or bad at." His face was close to hers. "We'll figure it out as we go along."

"Okay, I like that. But listen, I don't want you thinking you need to be perfect. If you're not being honest with me by being yourself, we have a problem. I don't want perfect. I want you." She poked her finger into his chest.

"In that case, I'm happy to tell you that I'm far from perfect. No need to worry about that." One corner of his mouth rose in a smile. "Can I kiss you now?"

"I thought you'd never ask."

As soon as his lips claimed hers, fireworks burst over her heart. Never in her wildest dreams did she think she'd end up with this cowboy. He'd always seemed a little too good to be true.

The reality?

He was even better than she'd imagined. And he was all hers.

Chapter Fifteen

Later that night, Cade carried a sleepy Tulip in one arm as he held Mackenzie's hand. They ascended the porch steps to his house. Ty's truck was parked in the drive, and from the delicious smells wafting from the back deck, he guessed Ty and Mom were grilling steaks. Cade had asked his brother to stop over. He and Mackenzie wanted to be together to share the good news that they were dating.

They'd already stopped by Patrick's house. Her father had grilled Cade along the lines of *why do you think you're good enough for my daughter?* (he knew he wasn't) and *if you hurt her, you'll have me and Charger to answer to* (no thanks). By the end of the visit, Patrick had given Cade an aggressive half hug with a clap on the back and told them he was happy for them.

"How do you think she'll react?" Mackenzie chewed on the corner of her lower lip.

"Imagine a shaken champagne bottle being uncorked." He gave her hand a squeeze. "That's a mere fraction of the happiness my mom will display."

"Are you sure? What if she doesn't think I'm the right person for you?"

"She already loves you." They reached the door. "Remember the Fourth of July? She would have gladly planned our wedding right there next to the ketchup and mustard stand."

"I don't know. I'm nervous."

"Don't be." He stopped on the welcome mat and turned to face her. "She's been waiting for me to have a serious girl-friend for years."

Her eyebrows rose as if she wanted to believe him but couldn't quite bring herself to.

Cade opened the door. "We're here."

He set Tulip down—the dog went straight to her bed—then led Mackenzie through the living room and kitchen to the dining area. Mom and Ty were out on the deck, and Mom held a spatula in the air as she talked. Ty looked like he was on the receiving end of a lecture.

The glass door slid open easily. Cade waited for Macken-zie to walk through. "It smells great out here."

Ty widened his eyes at him as if to say *finally*.

"Mackenzie!" Spatula still in hand, Mom threw her arms around her and hugged her tightly. "I'm so glad you can join us for supper." She looked at Cade and beyond him. "Where's Tulip?"

"Sleeping inside. That dog is tired."

"Oh, yeah?"

"I took her to see Nana, and she loved her."

"She was having a good day?" Mom's forehead wrinkled in concern. "I hate when I miss visiting her. But I promised the girls I'd help box donation items for the church rum-mage sale."

"You're at the nursing home every day, Ma," Cade said. "It's fine. And, yes, Nana was having a good day. You would have been proud of Tulip. She did everything right."

Mom clasped the spatula to her chest. "I'm so glad."

Ty grunted. "I need the spatula."

She thrust it his way.

"Before we eat, we have something to tell you." Cade glanced over at Mackenzie and wrapped his arm around her shoulders.

His mother's eyes grew as round as a full moon. "*We* have something to tell?" Her voice grew squeaky at the end.

"Yes," he said. "We're dating."

"Praise God!" Mom lifted her face to the sky and clapped her hands together. Was she about to cry? Then she opened her arms wide. Cade prepared himself for her hug, but she pushed past him to embrace Mackenzie.

Cade shot Ty a look, and Ty laughed. Loudly.

"See how you rank, bro?" Ty pointed the spatula to Mackenzie and back to Cade. "Get used to it."

He shook his head.

"I'm so glad you're taking a chance on my son. Now you come over anytime, okay, hon? Any. Time. I mean it. You can have supper with us every night if you'd like. Oh, and I have another book for you. You know what? I'll give you this month's, too. You can never have too much romance, now, can you?"

"Um, no?" Mackenzie had a shell-shocked look about her. Cade grinned. She was more than capable of handling Christy Moulten on her own. He'd give her time to adjust.

"That's right," Mom said. "And have you been over to Winston Ranch?"

"I have."

"Good." Mom nodded rapidly. "Then you've seen the Winston—the new event center perfect for weddings. I'll call Erica and have her give you a tour."

"We aren't engaged, Ma." Cade rolled his eyes.

"I know that." She had on her exasperated tone. "I'm just saying it wouldn't hurt to give it a look."

Ty's shoulders were shaking with laughter.

"This is the best day!" She actually hopped in place. "We need to celebrate!"

Cade took Mackenzie's hand and tugged her close to his side. "If you haven't noticed by now, Mom is big on celebrating."

"Life can be hard." Christy's chin soared. "We need to celebrate all the good times while we have them."

"I can't argue with that." He kissed Mackenzie's temple and dropped her hand. "Don't I get a hug, Mom?"

"Oh! I forgot!" She bustled to him and gave him a long embrace. "You did good, son."

"Thank you." They shared a loving look. "For everything."

She patted his cheek and turned to Ty. "Where are we at on this food?"

"Five more minutes. I'm not eating raw meat."

"Good. I'll fix us up some sparkling lemonade." She hurried inside the house.

Ty handed Cade the spatula. What was with everyone passing around the spatula? "What do you want me to do with this?"

"Hold it while I congratulate your girlfriend," Ty said.

"Oh, okay."

Ty hugged Mackenzie. "You've got a good one here."

"I know." She grinned.

"And he knows he's blessed to have you."

"Thank you."

"Now give me back my spatula."

Cade tossed it to him, and he caught it.

"Here we are." His mom appeared with a tray. She set it on the patio table and handed each of them a sparkling lemonade. "To Cade and Mackenzie. May you fall more in love each day. Cheers!"

"Cheers!"

As he clinked glasses with Mackenzie, he mouthed *I love you*.

She blushed.

"I saw that." Mom waggled her finger between them. She picked up two books from the tray. "Here you go, Mackenzie. This top one features quadruplet toddlers. I'm not trying to give you ideas. But I am going to call Erica right now to book you and Cade a tour of the Winston."

Cade opened his mouth to argue, then thought better of it.

As far as he was concerned, his mom was right. The sooner he could spend the rest of his life with Mackenzie, the better.

Epilogue

September's Jewel River Legacy Club meeting was getting lively, and he hadn't even made his big announcement yet.

Cade caressed Mackenzie's hand as she sat next to him. Normally, he came to these meetings solo, but she'd agreed to join him tonight. That way they could tell everyone their big news. Currently, Erica stood at the podium navigating old business, and it was going about as well as could be expected.

"We need to talk about last month's Shakespeare-in-the-Park film," Erica said, smiling at Angela Zane. "Angela, Joey and Lindsey did a phenomenal job. The production was top-notch."

"Are you going to mention the raccoon disaster, or do I have to?" Clem interrupted.

Cade personally thought the raccoons *had* been a problem. Apparently, Lindsey had forgotten to tell Joey she'd brought the trio of raccoons featured in the film to the actual festival. Someone's kid had opened the cage, and during the movie's finale, they'd scattered onto the lawn, where everyone was sitting on blankets.

"Lindsey admitted her mistake," Erica said calmly. "She should have had a lock on the cage. Plus, she realized she'd made the wrong decision by not discussing her plan with Joey."

"Rabies!" Clem yelled. His arms were locked under his chest. "Someone could have gotten rabies!"

"They're clean raccoons, Clem," Angela said brightly. "None of them have rabies."

"None that you know of." He glared at her.

Mackenzie rose. "I checked each raccoon before filming began, and they were all healthy. No rabies. Linda Roth domesticated them from birth and has them up to date with their shots."

Clem made a sucking sound with his teeth and raised his gaze to the ceiling in disgust.

"Those little animals added a lot of excitement." Angela waved one hand in dismissal. "No one was expecting the film to come to life, so to speak."

Cade glanced at Mackenzie. She appeared to be suppressing laughter. He leaned in and whispered, "You laugh now, but that night when everyone was worried about rabies and calling you for guidance, you weren't laughing."

"True."

"Anyway," Erica said loudly, "besides the raccoon incident, the film was a success."

"The kettle corn is always a hit, Erica," Mary Corning said. "When are we going to make it a permanent feature in the park?"

Erica's face pinched as she held on to her smile. "We can't. It's a health-code issue. Remember? But if we can continue relying on your crew to run it, we'll make sure there's kettle corn at all our major events."

The meeting continued, and nervous energy built inside Cade. When Erica asked if anyone had anything to add, he started to rise.

But his mom beat him to it.

What was she doing? Was she going to steal their thunder? Cade clenched his jaw. She'd better not.

"I could use some help," Christy said, standing on the

other side of Mackenzie. "I've decided to move to town soon. If any of you know anyone who is putting up their house for sale or even for rent, let me know. I need to be within walking distance of the nursing home and the supermarket."

Cade sat there as stunned as could be. Why hadn't she mentioned moving to him?

"Did you know about this?" Mackenzie frowned.

"No."

"You're moving to town, huh?" Clem leaned forward, searing Christy with his gaze.

"Yes, and I don't need any of your snide remarks."

"Point taken." He gave her a nod. "I tell you what. I'll teach you how to drive. I mean it. We'll go over all the things that you're doing wrong. Then you won't keep getting your license suspended, and you'll be able to get yourself around."

With his eyes wide, Cade leaned over to catch his mom's reaction. To his shock, she didn't explode. She simply nodded with her lips in a thin line.

"Thank you, Clem. I'll keep that in mind." She looked around the table. "Like I said, I'm actively house-hunting, so text or call me if you know a place going on the market."

"We'll do that," Erica said with a smile. "Anyone else have news?"

Cade stood. "Uh, yes. I do. We do. Over the weekend, Mackenzie agreed to marry me. I'm a blessed man."

Cheers and hollers erupted around the table. When they died down, he continued. "And Moulten Stables is officially open. I have four horses to rent for anyone who'd like to ride. They're suitable for the rodeo team if you've got some high-schoolers interested. The rates are low, so give me a call."

He sat again, and Mackenzie grinned at him, squeezing his hand.

His new stables were almost full. Forestline Adventures

had signed a contract to board all their horses with him this winter. The horses would be arriving by the middle of next month. Trent Lloyd had moved into the old house across the road from Moulten Stables, and he was as obsessed with horses as Mom was with weddings. Trent was turning out to be a great manager.

Best of all, Cade had the prettiest, smartest, most incredible woman by his side. Every night, they had supper together if Mackenzie wasn't out on a call. He couldn't wait to make her his wife.

The meeting adjourned, and several members stopped by to congratulate them. When everyone started clearing out, Cade found his mother.

"Why didn't you say anything to me about moving? I hope our engagement didn't bring this on."

"It didn't." Mom gave him a tender smile. "It's been on my mind for a while. I'm too far away from town. I want to be closer to my friends. Now that I have Tulip, I'm ready for my next adventure. She's a good companion."

That she was. He'd gotten in the habit of taking Tulip around to some of the other nursing home residents after visiting Nana. They all loved the dog. Some of them cried every time they petted her. It moved him, knowing how one little Pomeranian could positively impact so many lives.

Mackenzie stood next to him. "Are you going to let Clem help you with driving?"

"I might." Mom shrugged. "What have I got to lose at this point? My license?"

They all laughed.

"Come on," Cade said. "Let's get out of here."

The three of them walked outside. Clem was waiting on the sidewalk. "Christy, can I have a word?"

"Sure, Clem." Mom went over to talk to him.

Cade took the opportunity to put his arm around Mackenzie's shoulders. "I love you, you know."

"I know." She gave him a sideways grin. "Not as much as you love my mobile vet trailer."

"I do love it. All those gadgets. Makes a guy like me want to touch them all."

"What's mine is yours."

He spun her to face him. "And I'm all yours. Forever."

"You'd better be."

"You might regret those words."

"A lifetime with you? I'll never regret it."

Neither would he. He'd found the love of his life, and he'd never let her go. His heart was hers. Forever.

* * * * *

If you enjoyed this Wyoming Legacies story,
be sure to pick up the previous books in
Jill Kemerer's miniseries:

The Cowboy's Christmas Compromise
United by the Twins

Available now from Love Inspired!

And also check out the free online read
about Charlene's daughter, Janey,
"The Christmas Cowboy Next Door."
Available on Harlequin.com!

Dear Reader,

Are you a pet lover? I haven't met a dog, cat or bunny I haven't fallen in love with. As I was writing this book, I found myself wanting a sweet Pomeranian, too. They are such cute dogs. My elderly mini dachshund, Sophie, is my writing buddy. While she's not a therapy dog, she does comfort me often. Dogs are special that way.

My heart goes out to anyone with a loved one who has dementia and/or Alzheimer's. My father suffered from both, and watching it progress produced a steady stream of pain for everyone involved. I could relate to Cade's worry about wanting Tulip to get certified as a Canine Good Citizen in time to help his grandmother. But I also know God's timing is perfect. It's never too late to help someone in need, even if it doesn't look exactly the way we want it to.

I hope you enjoyed this book in the Wyoming Legacies series. I love connecting with readers. Feel free to email me at jill@jillkemerer.com or write me at P.O. Box 2802, Whitehouse, Ohio, 43571.

Blessings to you,
Jill Kemerer

HARLEQUIN
Reader Service

Enjoyed your book?

Try the perfect subscription for Romance readers and get more great books like this delivered right to your door.

See why over 10+ million readers have tried Harlequin Reader Service.

Start with a Free Welcome Collection with free books and a gift—valued over $20.

Choose any series in print or ebook. See website for details and order today:

TryReaderService.com/subscriptions